DEATHWIND

Andrea + Thom —

Gladys wanted me to
write a novel — so I did.
Not a good one, of course, but
the best I could do!

Don

DEATHWIND

Don C. Force

Northwest Publishing, Inc.
Salt Lake City, Utah

Deathwind

This is a work of fiction.
All characters and events portrayed in this book are fictional,
and any resemblance to real people or incidents is purely coincidental.

For information address: Northwest Publishing, Inc.
6906 South 300 West, Salt Lake City, Utah 84047
J. B. 2-10-95
C. R.

PRINTING HISTORY
First Printing 1996

ISBN: 1-56901-495-7

NPI books are published by Northwest Publishing, Incorporated,
6906 South 300 West, Salt Lake City, Utah 84047.
The name "NPI" and the "NPI" logo are trademarks belonging to
Northwest Publishing, Incorporated.

PRINTED IN THE UNITED STATES OF AMERICA.
10 9 8 7 6 5 4 3 2 1

To
Francie

Acknowledgments

The author is grateful to Dr. Lucile Jones, U.S. Geological Survey, Pasadena; Richard Chase and Morris McCutchin, both retired from the U.S. Forest Service Fire Laboratory, Riverside; and John Bryant, U.S. Forest Service, FIRESCOPE, Riverside. These good people gave their time to tell me what I needed to know.

ONE

Dr. Janice Ballard sat down wearily under one of several medium sized trees that provided the only real shade in the entire area. She removed her broad-brimmed hat, mopped her face and hat sweatband with a handkerchief, then laid the hat beside her on the ground. She undid the top button of her shirt to let the air circulate more freely. Her watch indicated 11:47 A.M. It was a hot September 12th. She had been thinking about shade for at least the last two hours, ever since the sun had begun to bear down with blazing intensity on the chaparral where she had been working since early that morning. There was precious little shade to be found in the brushy, shoulder-high vegetation that formed the chaparral. Luckily, there was a small stream—dry this time of year—situated near today's work site. The intermittent water supported the growth of a few trees even though the soil was rocky and shallow.

She called to her two assistants who were out of sight. It was time for lunch. Phil Granger was a tall, skinny redhead, who was the graduate student of another professor at the university. He had been studying certain chaparral birds for the last couple of years and was nearly ready to begin writing his master's thesis. Susan Shigawa was a second generation Japanese-American girl, short and thickset with a not un-pretty, but almost square appearing face. Susan had obtained her bachelor's degree last spring and was scheduled to start graduate school under Janice's guidance when fall term began in a few days. Susan was extremely intelligent and Janice felt lucky to have her as a graduate student. Both students had been working off and on for Janice the past several months. Lately she had begun to suspect more than just a "working" relation-ship between the two since they had more and more elected to work together, and very often out of her vision. She didn't really care as long as the work got done and the data they collected were reliable. The two would bear watching, how-ever, so that things didn't get out of hand. Screwing around in the chaparral was one thing; messing up scientific data was another.

Janice grinned to herself as she tried to picture a chaparral romance. How would it be consummated with any degree of passion or even comfort in such austere, miserable surround-ings? Would they make love on the rocky, baking-hot surface under the drappled half-sun, half-shade of a sparsely leafed manzanita bush perhaps? Could even the youngest and most ardent lovers find that endurable? She couldn't imagine how. In any event, she really wasn't that interested in young love; she was much more interested in how the information for her research project was gathered. Perhaps she would have to speak to them.

Janice Ballard had been a member of the Zoology faculty at California State since 1981. She had done her graduate work and obtained a Ph.D. at Berkeley. Her parents, espe-cially her mother, had been astounded that she would choose entomology as her life work. As she looked back on her life, however, she herself was not surprised the least bit. She recalled that animals interested her for as long as she could remember. Not just furry, cuddly animals, but all kinds—worms, spiders, snakes, frogs, slugs—all had been fascinating. She had been led into the world of insects by a particularly adept, young university instructor. Maybe she had even had some tender feelings for him. In any event, it was not uncommon these days for women to become entomologists. After Berkeley she had worked for industry a couple of years, but found that she hated the constriction of the industrial workplace. She felt extremely fortunate to have been chosen as a member of the faculty at California State. She realized that her sex hadn't in the least acted as a deterrent in procuring the appointment. On the other hand, she felt she had been highly qualified for the position regardless of her gender.

A head with short cropped red hair mostly hidden by a hat, a sharp prominent nose and rather large ears appeared over the hill. In a moment another head on a shorter frame also appeared; this one with long, black hair and soft, concave oriental features.

"Come sit beside me in the shade," Janice invited. Both assistants looked hot and tired. The invitation was accepted with obvious relief.

"Seems hotter today than yesterday," observed Phil, two thirds of his long-sleeved shirt was darkened with perspiration.

"It *is* hotter," Janice agreed. "The weatherman says a Santa Ana is due, perhaps tomorrow. I'd like to finish working this spot before the wind starts blowing. Maybe it will hold off a little longer. No use trying to collect insects in a wind. They stay pretty much hidden."

Phil was removing his boots. It was the first thing he did when coming to rest Janice had noticed. His boots came off first, then his hat, then his shirt. Janice had the feeling that as a kid he had gone barefooted most of the time, and would still like to.

"You guys see anything interesting today?" inquired Janice.

"We saw a lot of bees," replied Susan, looking at Phil for confirmation.

"We found a clearing where ground-nesting bees were making nests," said Phil. "Must have been thousands of bees, all very busy running in and out of their little holes in the ground." Grinning, he added, "Would have made a good meal for a flock of birds that like to eat bugs." Phil, as usual, was teasing Janice and Susan regarding his personal opinion, comparing the relative importance of birds with insects.

Janice Ballard liked university teaching and was good at it. Students instinctively warmed to her relaxed approach to teaching, but they also understood that she considered it her duty to teach them as much as possible about things she felt were important for them to know. She taught several courses dealing with insects and other invertebrate animals. She also conducted several research projects on a variety of insects in their natural habitats. One of these projects had to do with chaparral insects. She had been spending considerable time lately on this particular project because she was tired of the work and she wanted to finish and get something published. Originally she had been funded by the National Science Foundation, but her grant had run out and N.S.F. had been unable to provide her with more money. Now she was down to the last few hundred dollars of a small grant given her by the U. S. Forest Service. She had just enough left to pay her two helpers a few more weeks' wages.

Janice was in her late thirties and had two children to care for. Todd was in his early teens, the result of a broken marriage. The other was the pride of her life, a nine-year-old daughter, Jennifer, who was produced from an affair with a man she had met while doing summer research. She had been camping with Todd, who was six at the time, in the mountains of Arizona. Her field research project had just begun, and she was attempting to establish a daily routine whereby she could study her insect populations and keep an eye on Todd at the same time. About a week after she had set up camp, a gray camper truck had driven up. The driver was lost and needed directions. One thing led to another, and Richard decided to spend the remainder of the summer camped nearby. Jennifer was born nine and a half months after Richard had appeared. Richard was a high school teacher who enjoyed camping during summer vacation and was not interested in settling down or taking on responsibilities. So it began and ended all within two months' time.

The out-of-wedlock baby had presented no real problems for Janice except a few weeks' loss of wages. She had gone to her department chairman and asked for a short leave-of-absence without pay. Dr. Michaels' eyebrows had shot skyward when she explained the reason for the leave request. She was not surprised at his reaction. The chairman was in certain respects molded from an earlier generation. A nice older man who did his job and was generally well liked by the faculty, but who was governed by a more fastidious set of ethics. Michaels never mentioned the baby again as far as Janice could remember. Not even when Jennifer was born. No call to ask how mother and daughter were doing, no card, nothing. The remainder of the faculty had been more supportive.

It was getting hotter in the shade where Janice and her two companions were enjoying an after lunch siesta. Janice was trying to work out a program for the afternoon. Her watch said 12:42 P.M.

"Let's work till three," she suggested to Phil and Susan. After that, they still had nearly an hour of steep climbing to get back to the road where the car was parked. That was probably all she could expect from her helpers for one day.

She continued, "I'd like to stay longer because of the Santa Ana wind forecast, but perhaps if we get back early enough tomorrow morning, we can finish before the wind picks up." Janice could tell by the looks between Phil and Susan that they had hoped the afternoon would end even earlier. However, they agreed and Phil reluctantly began putting his boots back on.

Janice stood up and walked over to where she could look

southwestward out over the San Gabriel Valley and greater Los Angeles basin. A layer of brown was slowly rising from the valley floor like some grotesque amoeba, irresistibly enveloping the base of the San Gabriel Mountains lower down than where she stood. Later in the afternoon the brown monster would reach the 3600 foot level where they were working. The first indication would be the familiar, slightly acrid smell. With luck, they might be well up the mountainside on their way to the car before the smog caught up with them. Janice detested the heat and smog. Sometimes she wished she had looked harder for some sort of position at Berkeley where the air was nearly always cool and clean.

Janice strapped her plastic snake guards over the calves of her legs. The guards were hot and uncomfortable, but they also gave her some peace of mind. Rattlesnakes were common in the chaparral, and usually the brush was so thick that it was impossible to see where each step would lead. Besides, the snake guards saved a lot of wear and tear on her jeans. She wished she had been able to convince Phil and Susan to wear their own guards, but she had argued in vain. Both had maintained that the guards were too hot and cumbersome, and that it was easier to just be careful where one stepped. She had said nothing, but thought to herself that there was probably another explanation than the one they gave. Life to young people just wasn't worth the trouble unless there was a certain amount of risk involved. She probably had felt the same way when she was younger.

Just the same, she could not help being anxious about the situation, particularly in Phil's case. He had not advertised the fact by any means, but she had overheard him telling Susan one day that he was allergic to horse serum. This meant that if he were bitten by a snake, a shot of antivenin would be out of the question since it was produced from horses. He would have to take his chances without the treatment, and at very best, would be pretty sick. Perhaps she was being overly concerned. She had talked to some of the Forest Service people who worked in chaparral. They said the only snake bite they had experienced in their group was to a young man who was riding in a pickup truck. He had his arm extended out of the window as the truck was passing by an embankment about window high. The road was very rough and narrow and the embankment was close to the truck. A snake was coiled on the edge and struck the man's hand as the truck passed by. Oh well, she thought, such is the uncertainty of life, but it still pays to be careful.

The heat enfolded Janice as she picked up her backpack and insect net, and stepped out into the sun. Phil and Susan were headed off in an easterly direction along the side of the mountain. Janice decided to work westerly up and over a small ridge that led into a narrow ravine. It would be stifling in the ravine with no breath of a breeze, but the afternoon would be short. She would get engrossed in her work and the time would go quickly. Her body longed for the "fix" of a cigarette, but she tried to ignore it. It was the one vice in her life that she would have liked to control and had been unable to. She didn't even bring cigarettes or a lighter into the chaparral because of the fire danger. She would just have to wait until she got back to the safety of the car where there would be time for a quick smoke before they left.

She entered the ravine and began sweeping the brush with her net, periodically stopping to see what insects the net had trapped. Insects were hard to find in the middle of the day because many would be resting underneath leaves and other places out of the sun. However, she applied herself and soon lost track of time.

Suddenly she froze. She heard it coming before she felt it. She knew instantly what it was when the rumbling began because she had experienced several in the last few years. She could remember only one that made no sound before it hit.

Dear God, let it be a small one, she thought to herself as she always did when she heard the ominous sound.

The ground lurched feebly a couple of times, several miniature earth slides skittered down the sides of the ravine, and the earthquake was over. She glanced at her watch. It was

2:18 P.M. Jennifer would probably be on her way home from school. Jennifer was always frightened during earthquakes, but her mother had talked to her about them and tried to explain what was happening to the earth at such times. Janice decided that she and Jennifer would talk about earthquakes again tonight before bedtime.

TWO

Janice drove directly to the university after leaving the mountains. Susan had books and other stuff, she said, to pick up before going home, and Phil was just looking for some solitude to think about his thesis. Janice wanted to get her mail and check the telephone tape before leaving for home. She also wanted to speak to Tony Rogers about a class they were scheduled to team-teach when the fall term began in a few days. She thought Tony might still be at school since he had told her earlier in the week that he intended to spend several days analyzing some research data on his computer.

Janice always approached her mailbox with a faint feeling of anticipation, as if something exciting might be hiding there. Probably a holdover from earlier days when good things appeared in the mail occasionally—like a job offer, or a letter from the National Science Foundation saying she had been awarded a grant. Those days seemed to be over. Janice had not even tried to write a grant proposal to N.S.F. for the past several years. She had become convinced that N.S.F. would never again fund her research, at least not her chaparral research. Things had changed since earlier years. Money was tighter now. But she felt there might be other reasons.

The National Science Foundation sent proposals that it received from applicants out to a number of reviewers—usually about seven. The reviewers rated the proposals from poor to excellent. Nowadays, unless nearly all the reviews were rated very highly, there was little chance of being funded. Janice often wondered whether having nearly all excellent ratings depended entirely on the quality of the proposal. It seemed rather curious that she would consistently receive two or three excellent ratings and the rest mediocre. Either a proposal was excellent or it wasn't. Why this diversity? She had thought of a possibility or two.

First, she had always been pretty much of a loner in her research. The trend now was to award grants to a team of investigators working cooperatively. Second, very few scientists were working in the area of chaparral insects. She knew perhaps two persons who were well enough acquainted with her work to adequately judge its quality. That was not enough. Evaluators working in other areas were reluctant to give top ratings regardless of the quality of the proposal. Often they did not recognize its quality or importance, or they were simply not that interested in the research. She wondered, also, whether the "good old boy" syndrome was a factor—you rate my proposal highly and I'll do the same for you. She had no evidence at all. She felt there was no way to improve her proposals, and rewriting them every year was a waste of time and effort.

There appeared to be nothing interesting in her mailbox from a quick run-through, but she folded everything together so it could be stuffed into her briefcase for a more careful analysis later.

Tony Rogers was busy talking to a young woman Janice did not recognize as she passed the open door of his office. She decided to pick up some lecture notes in her own office before checking on Tony again. She needed to spend some time revising the notes of one of her courses before teaching it again this coming year. She would have to take some time away from her field work to do this.

After unlocking her office door, she checked the phone message light. It was blinking. She punched in the message access number. Janice was pretty sure the message would be from one of her kids. They knew she would be stopping at school before coming home. The message was from Todd, informing her that he was at the home of one of his friends and would be eating dinner there. He would be home later in the evening. That meant she had to hurry now so she could pick up Jennifer before it got too late. Jennifer stayed with a neighbor lady in the afternoon after school when Todd wasn't home.

Janice decided there wasn't time now to talk to Tony. Perhaps she could phone him this evening. Dr. Anthony Rogers had come to Cal State three years after she had. He was from Ohio and seemed to have adapted rather well to Southern California. He also did research work on "little creatures" as he called them, but his interest was with marine bivalves instead of insects. He spent much of his time at the beach or in the ocean. He was an accomplished scuba diver.

Tony was several years younger than Janice and had never married. He seemed only casually interested in women, dated occasionally but never became serious about anyone in particular. He took Janice out once in a while, but the relationship was, so far at least, totally without signs of romantic intent. She wondered at first if he would eventually get around to asking if she wanted to climb into bed with him, but she had misjudged him. Janice now considered Tony to be simply a good friend—perhaps as good a friend as she had. He often took Todd to the beach and was instructing him in the fundamentals of scuba diving. Todd enjoyed being with Tony and Janice felt that her son was in good hands.

Janice also got along well with Tony, although they were not without occasional differences. One subject they could not agree on was the effect of the massive number of immigrants coming into Southern California. Many of them were entering illegally. Hundreds, perhaps thousands of Mexicans and other Latinos came surging across the California border every night, spreading like a massive cancer. In Janice's view, California would become an extension of Third World poverty. They would not stop coming until Mexico was a better place to live than the United States. One could hardly tell where Mexico ended and California began. These illegals were usually uneducated and unskilled, without money, and the women bore lots of kids.

Tony was not nearly as pessimistic about the situation. Janice thought his attitude might have something to do with his coming from the Middle West. He had not grown up in California and could not comprehend the scope of changes that had taken place over the years. He did not understand what California had been like at one time. She thought another reason for his naiveté might be the community in which he had settled. He was not seeing what she saw because he lived in a far different environment. Tony had never been in need of money. His parents were well-to-do and had simply given him the down payment on a moderately expensive home in Claremont, one of the affluent communities resting at the very base of the San Gabriel Mountains, east of Los Angeles.

When Janice had purchased her home, she felt she could not afford a place in one of these more exclusive areas. She was forced to purchase farther south in Pomona, away from the mountains, where prices were lower. Her area was now being inundated by Latinos. There were times at the supermarket when Janice did not hear a single customer conversing in anything but Spanish. One could get along perfectly well in Southern California without speaking a word of English. These people moved to a new land, but wanted to keep their own culture and language. Janice felt the schools her children attended were rapidly deteriorating. She had noticed a big change in the past several years. The majority of kids weren't interested in school, and their parents often seemed even less interested. The schools were badly overcrowded. Juvenile gangs were everywhere. Janice had no personal animosity toward any of these people and she understood their motives, but she felt they were destroying the system.

Tony did not see these problems. He shopped in supermarkets where the clientele was predominately white and well off. The schools in his community were still teaching higher math classes and giving homework at night. Janice and Tony lived in different worlds. She wondered what would eventually happen to both worlds. She wasn't sure she wanted to stay to find out. She wondered whether there might be a better and healthier place to raise her children, away from the smog, the ever increasing congestion, the gang fights, the graffiti, the overcrowded freeways, the danger of being out on the streets at night…, but maybe she was just tired.

Jennifer and Janice were greedily devouring TV dinners that evening, sitting on the floor and watching a program about African animals on the television set. Occasionally they ate dinner in this casual manner when they were by themselves. When all three were home together, Janice tried to be a little more formal and they would eat around the table with the television turned off. At this time they could discuss the day's events, or bring up problems or items of interest. It was the only time they had for this kind of activity.

Janice thought it was a little strange that Jennifer had not even mentioned the afternoon's slight earthquake. Usually her daughter could talk of nothing else after such an event. Janice wasn't sure she wanted to bring the subject up, but she was curious about Jennifer's behavior. Perhaps she could just ask Jennifer if she had felt it. Janice turned the television down a little so she could talk.

"Jennifer," she began, "did you feel that little earthquake this afternoon?"

Jennifer looked at her mother a little strangely. "An

earthquake?" she responded. "There wasn't no earthquake this afternoon, Mom. I would have felt it if there was."

"Honey, it was just a little one. Probably it happened when you were on your way home from school. You didn't feel anything?"

Jennifer thought a moment. "By the way, Mom, I felt a little dizzy once on my way home, like that time I was getting the flu. I just bent over till I felt better."

Janice grinned. "Did your feet seem like they were moving without your wanting them to?"

Jennifer turned from the television to her mother. "I thought I might fall over for a second, Mom, that's all."

"That was the earthquake, Jennifer. It made the ground move so you thought you were getting dizzy."

Jennifer smiled, then laughed out loud. "Mom, I must be getting used to them. They don't scare me no more."

Janice smiled too, then became more serious. "The little ones aren't very scary, sweetheart. Let's hope they are all little ones from now on."

Jennifer raised up on her knees with a slightly frightened look on her face. "Will there be more, Mom?"

"We live in a place where there are earthquakes once in a while. Remember the talk we had about them several months ago? I hope we won't have any more, but I'm pretty sure we will. That's the way it is here in this place."

"Can't we move, Mom?" Jennifer asked.

Her mother smiled. "Yes, we could move. But there are bad things anywhere you go. Do you recall the evening we were talking to Tony about where he used to live? They have terrible wind storms there, remember? Tornadoes he called them. They can be pretty frightening too."

"Isn't there some place where nothing will hurt us?" asked Jennifer.

"Well, probably not. Life is like that. There are scary things almost everywhere."

Janice moved over and turned off the television. "I want to talk to you a little more about earthquakes," she said.

"Remember what I told you before about what you should do if there was a bad one? I know you're uncomfortable talking about them, Jennifer, but I have to be sure that you understand."

"You said to stay where I am and you will come as soon as you can," said Jennifer.

"Yes, that's what I told you. No matter where you are, stay put and try not to worry about me. I will come, but maybe not right away. That depends on where I am. If I'm out on a field trip or something it might be a whole day or two before I can get back to you. You must understand that, and not get frightened. You're to follow the instructions of whoever is taking care of you and be brave. Understand?"

"Okay, Mom, but I hope an earthquake doesn't ever happen again. And if it does, I'm leaving here and never coming back, whether you come with me or not." Jennifer was grinning her mischievous grin. Janice grabbed her and they hugged each other tightly.

Janice turned the television on softly again and stretched out on the floor. She was tired after climbing up and down mountains all day. There was a faint scratch at the screen door in back.

"Jennifer, honey, could you let the kitty in and give him some food, please? I'm really tired or I'd do it myself."

Jennifer sprang to her feet. "My kitty wants to see me! Come here, baby," she twittered.

Janice was surprised to find herself on a strange mountain. She was chasing a unique insect she had never seen before. She had forgotten to put on her snake guards, but for some reason it didn't seem to matter. She went crashing though the brush with little thought of snakes or anything else but the insect. There was only one problem. Every time she got close to her quarry and had her net ready to sweep down upon it, the earth rolled slightly and her prize was gone again. She was sweaty now and a little angry. Why did the earth have to shake every time she was ready to strike?

A faint, "Mom, what's the matter?" interrupted her anger. She woke with a start.

"Oh, I guess I was dreaming." She glanced sheepishly at Jennifer who was observing her with a worried look. "Thanks for waking me up, sweetheart. I was having sort of a bad dream."

"It's okay, Mom, everything's okay."

"Yes, I know, dear." Janice waited a moment until her head cleared, then got up. "I have to phone Tony now," she said. "I have to talk to him about something."

THREE

A very large, high pressure area was building over the Great Basin. The condition was not uncommon for September and for several months thereafter each year. September was usually the beginning of the season when Santa Ana winds could be expected in Southern California, and a high pressure system in the Great Basin was one of the conditions necessary for the winds to blow. What interested Gilbert Dillard, one of the meteorologists at the U.S. Forest Service Fire Laboratory in Riverside, were indications that a low pressure area was developing simultaneously off the coast of Southern California. The greater the difference between high and low pressures, the stronger the winds would blow.

It was September 12, slightly past 3:00 P.M. The fire weather forecaster at the University of California had just phoned with the information. She thought Dillard would be interested since he had recently published an article on Santa Ana winds in one of the meteorological journals. Apparently the article had come to the attention of the Los Angeles Times because a reporter had called for an interview. The result was a rather lengthy write-up in the Times, starting on page three of the front section and continuing sporadically for several pages among segments of other stories and advertisements for clothes, food, bank loans, stereo systems, and an array of other products. Anyone with enough interest and patience could read the whole thing simply by following the instructions indicating where to go next. Surprisingly, 85 percent of the article was correct.

There were two things Dillard detested about newspapers. One was their size. Newspapers were simply too large. They were too unwieldy to read comfortably while eating at a table unless you folded them a couple of times. They were, in fact, difficult to read anywhere. One had to extend one's arms out half their length just to open the things up. A smaller, more magazine-like size would be much more convenient. His other peeve was the way articles were broken into pieces. Why couldn't they just print an entire article on one page instead of sending the reader fumbling through a whole section, picking up bits and pieces here and there.

The *Times* seemed to be interested in only a limited portion of his original publication. It was the part that dealt with the vulnerability to fire of many populated communities in the Los Angeles basin and inland valley areas, particularly those communities bordering the foothills and mountains where chaparral grew and where Santa Ana winds blew. Apparently, the editors thought this was the only newsworthy part of the publication; ironically, the part that dealt with potential death and destruction. His point had been that under severe Santa Ana conditions, where northeast winds can reach forty to sixty, even eighty miles per hour, nearly all of the inland communities that were situated up against the south-western side of the San Gabriel Mountains, were potential fire bombs.

Dillard had been surprised that the *Times* was interested in his article. Perhaps they had been desperate for news just then. His news was surely neither novel nor surprising. There was ample past evidence that brush fires burning under windy conditions can easily enter housing areas and are nearly unstoppable. Let something happen to the water supply, and fire fighters are totally helpless. Even with water, the fire progresses so rapidly that often one fire engine has to be stationed by every home in order to protect it. There were numerous examples from the past, like the fires all over Southern California in 1993, the Oakland fire of 1991, the Santa Barbara fire of 1990, and the terrible fire storms in Southern California during late September and early October of 1970.

A Santa Ana wind can develop after a cool air mass from the Northern Pacific or Canada moves into the Great Basin and stagnates in this inter-mountain location. The stagnated air forms a high pressure mass. If a trough or low pressure center is located on the other side of the mountains along the coast of Southern California, the strong gradient will pull air over the mountains from the high to the low pressure area. Since the mountains block the flow of ground surface air from the Great Basin, the flow comes from upper air, which is dry and potentially warmer. On the Pacific side of the mountains, the pressure gradient forces local surface air away and re-places it with this fast inflowing Great Basin air, which warms still more as it descends, making it even drier. The resulting strong winds, warmer temperature and low humidities all produce hazardous fire conditions.

Dillard studied the situation intently. There was every indication that by tomorrow or the next day, a very strong Santa Ana condition would develop. There had been several dry years in Southern California in the recent past. This year there had been more rain, but that had just stimulated the growth of more brush and grass. As normal in California, there had been no precipitation since earlier in the spring. The grass was brown and dry. The chaparral on the lower slopes, which would burn almost any time except in a rain storm, was tinder-dry. It was ready to explode.

All of this Gilbert Dillard considered rather grimly. He picked up his pipe from the top of his desk and tapped the ashes out. He dug around inside the pipe bowl with a straightened paper clip to clean out the remaining ashes and tobacco. Then he removed the lid from the tobacco humidor on his desk and began refilling his pipe slowly and carefully. Filling and lighting his pipe was a routine that he performed several times a day and with a great deal of pleasure. He used to do it more often, but now they were not permitted to smoke in the offices. They had to go outside on the patio to light up. The smell and taste of freshly lit pipe tobacco was like the ambrosia of life for Dillard. Ten years ago, in his early fifties, he would have said that hunting or backpacking or skiing were what life was all about. Now, he was not so sure. A decade could make a lot of difference.

At one of the U.S. Geological Survey buildings located across the street from Caltech in Pasadena, Dr. Peter Chin was busy at his desk. It was 3:39 P.M. according to the clock on the wall, and there had been a small earthquake earlier that afternoon off to the northeast near the mountains. It had been large enough to be felt in Pasadena, however.

Chin was talking to himself about the absurdity of some new report forms he was in the process of filling out. Like most other governmental agencies, the Geological Survey did some stupid things. These new forms were completely unnecessary and inadequate for the purpose for which they were designed. They had undoubtedly been thought up at headquarters by some administrator who was completely out of touch. The forms would be dutifully completed by every field office for a couple of years and sent into headquarters, where they would be stored. When it became apparent even to the most dense of administrators that they were totally useless, a memorandum from headquarters would appear at each and every field office explaining that it was no longer necessary to complete and forward these forms. It would be recommended that supplies of unused forms be destroyed. Meanwhile, the completed forms at headquarters would sit around for several more years until the space they occupied was needed, then *they* would also be destroyed. Typical government procedure. Chin had been with the government only seven years, but he had seen it happen before.

This afternoon's earthquake had been sensed by over 300 seismic stations in Southern California. These stations were the outcome of a cooperative program between the Geological Survey and Caltech that began in the 1970's. It was called the Southern California Seismic Network. The sensors from the stations were picked up continuously on a Caltech computer that scanned for earthquakes. If the ground moved enough at enough different sites, the computer would trigger and record the event. A good estimate of the location and magnitude of the quake could be obtained in about four minutes if the disturbance was not too large. Today's quake epicenter was northeast of the city of Upland, along the Cucamonga fault. The magnitude was an estimated 4.6.

The Cucamonga fault was a part of what seismologists referred to as the Transverse Ranges Frontal fault. It ran parallel with the San Gabriel Mountains on their southwest boundary along the base of the range. West of the city of Claremont, running to San Fernando, it was called the Sierra Madre fault. East of Claremont, running right up to the larger and better known San Andreas fault at Cajon Pass, it had been named the Cucamonga fault. The Frontal fault had been increasingly active in recent years. Since it was located closer to the densely populated Los Angeles area, a smaller earthquake here could be potentially just as destructive as a larger one on the San Andreas.

The movement along the Frontal fault was always vertical. In fact, the San Gabriel Range was the result of seismic action. The mountains had been lifted over eons of time by being wedged upward by the crust of the Los Angeles basin.

In 1971 and early 1994, smaller faults in the same general system gave way, causing the Sylmar and Northridge earthquakes. Over the past few years, a series of moderate earthquakes had occurred, moving progressively northeastward under the San Gabriel Valley to the mountains. Seismologists were concerned that the progression was tracing an area of enhanced strain that could suddenly break into a large earthquake along the Sierra Madre and Cucamonga faults.

Peter Chin folded the report and stuffed it into an envelope. It was nearly 4:00 P.M. and time to go home. He remembered that he had to stop at the supermarket on the way. His wife had given him a grocery list that morning. She had said, "If you want dinner tonight, don't forget to pick these things up." He would get home before she did since she worked until five. He would start dinner and surprise her.

FOUR

Janice Ballard had a difficult time going to sleep that night. She lay in her bed, wide awake, as a whole series of thoughts went through her mind. She thought about her teaching position, her children, what she wanted to do with her life when her children were grown and gone, whether she would be lonely then, whether she was really satisfied with what she possessed and with what she was doing. Her discussion with Jennifer earlier in the evening had resurrected some doubts that had plagued her off and on for some time. Of course, Jennifer was just a child and didn't realize what she was saying, but her daughter's asking if there weren't some better place to live had hit a nerve in Janice's conscience. Were there really better places to live, or was it just a trade off; one kind of problem substituted for another?

Janice had tenure at the university and was solidly entrenched in her research projects. It would be difficult just to pick up and walk away from this part of her life. On the other hand, the California State University System was having extremely difficult budget problems. Student fees had risen dramatically. Temporary, part-time instructors, as well as some tenured faculty, had been laid off. Classes had been canceled because there was no money to pay teachers. Equipment could not be repaired or replaced. Teaching supplies could not be purchased. Preserved animal specimens for study in Janice's zoology laboratories had to be shared among many students because there were not enough to go around.

Other state institutions were just as bad off. The state of California was having to live on less money for many reasons. One reason seemed to be that the recession had lasted longer here than in most other states. Many middle and higher income people, who paid higher taxes, had moved away leaving retirees and immigrants with children who take more than they give. Some industries had moved out because it was cheaper to do business in other states and other countries. The aerospace industry had been devastated. The jobless rate was higher than in most other states. Welfare payments had been lowered some, but they were still higher than in other states.

Jennifer and Todd were attending schools where discipline and entertainment were substituted for education. Teachers could do little or nothing about the situation. Janice had thought about moving to some nearby community like the one where Tony lived. The schools were better there, but she could not see any way that she could afford the move. Housing was just too expensive in those areas.

Janice turned over in her bed once more. She simply *had* to get to sleep. She thought about Tony. She would probably like to marry someone like him. They had talked a long time on the phone earlier that evening. He was a real nice guy even if he had always had plenty of money. He had tired of the data processing that he had been doing all week and was heading for the ocean tomorrow to do some field research on his bivalve animals. He had invited Todd to come along if he wished. Todd was, of course, thrilled at the prospect when Janice mentioned it to him after he got home later in the evening. She would have to wake him early so he would be ready when Tony came by. Todd would miss a day of school, but he learned much more by being with Tony than he did at school. Jennifer would also have to rise a little earlier since Janice wanted to get back up into the chaparral as early as possible.

Janice had called Mrs. Lavin, Jennifer's sitter, and had made arrangements to drop her daughter off early. Mrs. Lavin would give Jennifer her breakfast and send her off to school. Mrs. Lavin, an elderly lady who had lost her husband just a couple of years ago, was indispensable. Jennifer was fond of her, and Mrs. Lavin simply loved Jennifer as if she were her granddaughter. The older lady was always eager for Jennifer to spend extra time with her, and she could probably use the extra money.

Finally, Janice gave up trying to go to sleep. She got up, put on her robe, got a cigarette from the pack she kept in her dresser drawer, and went out on the back patio. It was still warm outside. She never smoked inside the house anymore. Even though she had been unable to kick the cigarette habit completely, at least she would not contaminate her house with smoke. She didn't want her children to have to breathe cigarette smoke on top of the smog that they were exposed to for at least half the year. Smog—another reason for getting them out of this place. Maybe after she smoked her cigarette, she would read awhile and, hopefully, get sleepy before long. But her thoughts kept wandering. Sometimes she wished she could take her brain out at night and lay it on the shelf until morning. She had spent many sleepless nights simply because she could not turn off her thoughts.

Janice was lonelier than most of her friends knew. She had the children, of course, but they were no substitute for a man that she could love and be loved by in return. When she had been married, her husband could not be faithful to her as she demanded. And so he had tried to deceive her by denying his affairs with other women. They had married while they were both graduate students. Both had obtained research assistant-ships, and since they were living in university housing where rent was cheap, they got along on their combined incomes.

As soon as it was evident that Scott could not account for all the time he spent away from their apartment, Janice had begun to look into his activities. She had finally found several women, mostly other students, whom he had been going to bed with. She confronted him with the information she had gathered and he could not deny the truth. He said he would reform, but as time passed it became evident that he had no intention of doing so. She divorced him during her final year of graduate school, just before she had received her Ph.D. Todd had been born that same year. Scott had simply disap-peared, and Todd had never known his father. Janice's parents had helped her financially until she had found a job and became more stabilized. She owed her parents a great deal for their support during that time.

After finishing her cigarette, Janice went back into the house, found the novel she had been reading for several nights, and turned on the radio to an all-night classical music station. It would soon be 11:30 P.M. and she hoped she would be asleep by midnight. She opened her book but found she could not concentrate on the story. Her mind wandered back to her childhood and teenage years. She had never been particularly popular with her schoolmates. There had been very few close friends, and for the most part, she was considered to be a loner. It was very difficult for her to be at ease around people. Most people probably thought that she was standoffish and slightly conceited, but this was not at all true. More than anything, especially during her teenage years, she longed to be accepted by her peers and popular among them. She would have given anything to have a boy pay attention to her. But none ever did. And she was too shy to talk to them. Sometimes she had endured an unbearable ache—an unfulfilled desire to have a boyfriend that would love her and that she could love in return and have complete confidence in. She felt that high school had been a bad experience. She studied hard and got excellent grades, but detested most of it.

The university had been better. She became deeply interested in some of her subjects. Finally, in the middle of her sophomore year, she decided biology was what she wanted to do for the rest of her life. She took an insect course and was so fascinated that she took several more. She graduated with high honors and was accepted as a Ph.D. candidate by the entomology department. The next three years were the happiest of her life. She was totally engrossed in her studies and her part-time research assistantship. She met Scott in a graduate botany class. He was the first man other than her father to pay attention to her. When he asked her to marry him, she accepted instantly. It had been a mistake. She didn't know him at all.

A little noise in the house startled her. It was probably Jennifer.

"Jennifer, is that you?" she called softly.

"It's me, Mom. I had to go to the bathroom," Jennifer replied. She emerged from the hall squinting her eyes against the light.

"You're up late, Mom. You'll be cranky tomorrow," warned Jennifer.

"Come here and give me a big hug, young lady. It's just what I need to put me to sleep," said Janice.

Jennifer put her arms around her mother. Janice noticed how warm and soft she was.

"I love you, sweety," murmured Janice.

"I love you too, Mom."

As Jennifer padded back to her bedroom, Janice closed her book and went back to her own bed. She finally dropped off to sleep thinking again about Tony and how lovely it would be to have a little romance once again in her life with someone like him.

FIVE

"Todd, wake up!" Janice shook her son gently. It was slightly before 5:00 A.M., and Janice had been up for about 30 minutes getting dressed and making lunches. Todd would be fairly easy to get out of bed since he was excited about going with Tony. Jennifer might be more difficult. Janice would let her sleep a little longer so Todd could use the bathroom first.

"Todd, are you awake?" Janice called again through his closed door.

"I'm up, Mom, and half-dressed," answered Todd. He had carefully laid out the clothes he was going to wear before he went to bed the night before. Janice had packed three lunches with sandwiches, cookies and fruit. Everyone liked a different kind of fruit, so there was a banana in Jennifer's, two large apples in Todd's and red seedless grapes in her own. As far as she was concerned, red seedless grapes were the greatest miracle since the microwave oven. She never got tired of them although sometimes they were a little expensive.

The coffee was perking and the pancake batter was about ready.

"Todd, how long?" she called.

"About three minutes," he answered.

"Todd, go wake your sister before you come out to eat," she yelled. That would be the first call. Janice would have to call Jennifer at least two more times before anything much would happen. Jennifer woke up hard and was ugly for a few minutes before she decided that things weren't as bad as they seemed. Todd always woke up in a good mood.

"Jenny called me a name," announced Todd, "so I poked her."

"Okay," answered Janice. "Everything seems to be about normal so far this morning. I'm sure she'll have a name for me too when I go in there."

"She won't call you what she called me," said Todd, grinning. "Where does she pick up that kind of stuff? I was 12 or 13 before I knew what that meant."

Janice grunted. "She picks up all kinds of crap at school. Every now and then I have to dry-clean her vocabulary."

"Did you have to do that with me?" asked Todd.

"To a certain degree," answered Janice. "But, you were a little different."

"How?" Todd was genuinely curious.

"Well, you always had a lot of sense, even when you were real little. I don't know how to explain it, but some kids seem to be born sensible and others never do catch on. Must be a matter of genetics," answered Janice. She put a stack of pancakes on Todd's plate.

"Eat now, son. Tony will be here before you know it."

Janice poured herself a cup of coffee and made a quick trip into Jennifer's bedroom while the second batch of cakes were cooking. Jennifer had her pillow up over her head and was obviously not interested in getting up. Janice pulled the pillow off, threw the covers back and gave her daughter a not-too-hard smack on her bottom.

"Get up, you lazy thing, right now!" she ordered. There was no discernible response from the child, but Janice had to get back to the pancakes.

It's true, Janice thought as she turned the pancakes. Some kids are just easy and some are tough. Todd had never given her a bit of trouble. He had been unbelievably easy to rear, and she was eternally grateful for it. Many of his traits she could see in her own father. Todd was easygoing and very stable. She had never had to worry about him during any of his growing up period, at least so far. He just seemed to know that some things like drugs and early sex were bad and were to be left alone. Peer pressure was something that didn't appear to phase him. He was a real angel, and she was lucky above all reason to have a son like that. He could just as easily have been a hell raiser. She felt guilty that Jennifer was her favorite child, but she had tried very hard not too show it. She hoped that Todd had not guessed what her feelings were. Certainly Jennifer, with her personality, would be more of a handful as she got older than Todd would ever be.

Janice put another stack of cakes on Todd's plate.

"Is that enough, honey, or do you want some more?" she asked. "Drink your orange juice."

"That's all I want, Mom. I'm nearly full."

"You have 10 minutes before Tony will be here," said Janice. "Is the stuff you're taking all together? Don't forget to brush your teeth."

"Everything's ready and so am I," answered Todd. "Can I have a little money, Mom?"

"Bring my purse here and I'll see what I have." Todd had a part-time job, eight to ten hours a week when they needed him, but Janice was trying to get him to save most of the little bit of money he made. A honk out in front announced the early arrival of Tony. Janice hurried to the front door to signal Tony that they had heard.

"Want a cup of coffee before you go?" yelled Janice. Tony

shook his head and pointed at his watch. She waived and went back to check on Jennifer. She would have to hurry now to get Jennifer on her way and then herself to school where her two assistants would probably be waiting for her.

It was just after 6:00 A.M. when Janice got to the university. Both Phil and Susan had arrived earlier. It was already pretty warm; in fact, the night had never really cooled off normally. Today would be a scorcher. The weather forecaster on Channel 7 had predicted over 100 degree temperatures in the inland valleys. He had also indicated that the expected Santa Ana winds would begin to blow sometime during the day.

The drive up the mountain usually took 45 to 50 minutes. Their packs and equipment were already in the trunk of Janice's car, having been left there overnight. Susan quickly jumped into the front seat beside Janice and gave Phil a victory grin. Phil returned the grin with his favorite "ugly face" and climbed into the back seat.

"Hey, Dr. Ballard, do we get overtime pay or something for working on excessively hot days?" inquired Phil, winking at Susan, who had turned to look at him.

"Not unless you work overtime," answered Janice, smiling at Phil in the rear-view mirror.

"When does overtime start?" asked Phil.

"I'd say anything over 14 hours a day is overtime on this job," replied Janice.

"Just thought I'd ask," said Phil.

They rode in silence for a few minutes.

"How is your thesis coming, Phil?" asked Janice.

"I can't get started on it. I always have trouble starting papers. I never know what to write first."

"Have you talked to your major professor?" inquired Janice.

"Yeah, I talked to Dr. Edgarton and he gave me some ideas, but I'm still stuck. I'm not too crazy about any of them. After I get going I'll be okay. I've got lots of good data. Even Dr. Edgarton agrees with that."

"So, how long do you think it will take to finish the thesis and get ready for your oral exam?" asked Janice.

"Well, I was thinking about the first of the year, but I'm not sure I can do it by then," answered Phil. "And even if I do, is that a good time to start looking for a job? On the other hand, I'm not sure I can afford to wait around until spring when more jobs open up. My money situation is getting critical."

Janice had never questioned Phil about whether he was getting financial help from his parents or from any other source. She knew that he had worked at several jobs since coming to the university. She wished that she had more grant money to hire good students like Phil, and at the same time help get with her own research. Phil would have the proper papers to teach in a community college, but those jobs were hard to come by. Perhaps he would rather get some sort of research position with industry or a technician position with another university, or perhaps even something with the federal or state government. But not too many industries hired bird people, and government jobs were also hard to find. There was no money available to hire. Much federal and virtually all state hiring was frozen because of budget problems.

Janice turned to Susan. "How goes it with you, my friend?" she asked, giving Susan a lopsided smile. "Any regrets yet about your decision to do a research project under yours truly?"

"None whatever," replied Susan. "I'm really anxious to get started on something. And I know about what I want to do. I just have to work out the details."

"Have our little talks helped you any?" asked Janice.

"Oh, sure they have," replied Susan. You've given me some super ideas. So many of them sound interesting. That's part of the problem. They all sound good. I have to decide what I'm most interested in."

"Pick something you can do in a reasonable time," continued Janice. "This is only a masters' degree you're working for, not a Ph.D. You may want to go on for a Ph.D. somewhere else, say at Berkeley, for example."

Susan couldn't help grinning slightly at the mention of

Berkeley. Dr. Ballard was high on her own alma mater and was not reluctant in recommending it to students. In the back seat there was a snort from Phil. He and Janice had a continuous, good natured feud going about the quality of education at Berkeley. Not that Phil knew that much about it, but they both enjoyed the banter. Phil would argue about almost anything, but never appeared to get very serious. It was a game he loved to play. Janice turned and stuck out her tongue at him.

"She can't go to Berkeley," said Phil. "We've got an understanding."

Janice looked at Susan. "What's he talking about?" she asked in a slightly hesitant voice as though she were afraid of what the answer might be.

"Well—" said Susan, looking back at Phil.

"Maybe it's none of my business," Janice put in quickly.

"Oh, what the hell," exclaimed Phil. "Susan and I have some rather indefinite plans that we hope will work out for the best. We'd like to get married someday if there aren't too many obstacles—and maybe even if there are too many."

Janice stared in amazement at Susan. This was something totally unexpected. Sure, she had been speculating on whether some kind of affair was going on, but she never dreamed it was anything like this. After her surprise had subsided slightly she said, "Well, I suppose congratulations are in order."

"Not yet," replied Phil. "They're a little premature. Better wait till something happens. It may be quite a long time off."

"Does this affect your plans to work on your master's degree this coming year?" Janice asked Susan.

"Oh no, school comes first, always," replied Susan. "My parents would be devastated if marriage interfered with my schooling and I just can't do that to them."

Janice thought to herself about some of the stories she had heard concerning the adamant attitudes of some parents, and how they had led to misunderstandings with their children. Sometimes very bitter controversies developed which ended with the complete isolation of the children. Apparently, this was not to be the case here. She longed to ask Susan if her parents knew about Phil, but her better sense prevailed and she beat down the urge.

"Well, I'm a little flabbergasted," admitted Janice.

"We thought you would be," said Susan. "We debated about telling you, and finally decided not too. I guess old 'big mouth' in the back seat changed his mind and forgot to notify me." Susan shot Phil a disdaining look and tried to appear disgusted. Phil just grinned.

"What we don't want to happen is to be separated for long periods of time," observed Susan. "That seems to be pretty lethal to many engagements and marriages. If Phil got a job around here and I went far away someplace to school, there could be trouble. I guess we would each like to get a Ph.D. someday, but that will take some planning and probably some sacrifice. I'm sure we'd like to be together whatever we decide to do."

"I think togetherness is wise," replied Janice. "Will your parents help with the finances?"

"We haven't mentioned this to any of them," said Phil. "Nobody knows nuthin' and we want to keep it that way for a while." So Janice had the answer to the question she wanted to ask and hadn't, at least not directly. If Susan's parents knew about Phil at all, at least they didn't realize how serious the relationship was.

The drive up the mountain was beautiful as always. All three biologists enjoyed just looking at the passing scenery. The air was clear. There was no hint today of developing haze, which would later turn into smog. They turned off the main road onto a dirt, Forest Service road. The gate was locked but the Forest Service had given Janice a key. There was just the slightest indication of a breeze arising from the northeast. It was visibly stirring some of the shrub foliage and the dry grass along the road. Janice had been a little concerned about working today with the wind forecast. Of course, the forecast could be wrong, but probably wasn't. The whole trip might be a waste of time. The wind could begin to blow in an amazingly short time, and it would affect the insect collecting. The collecting data would be worthless if the wind began to blow hard much before noon.

"The plan for today will be for you two to work at the place where we collected last week," announced Janice. "You know, the spot where the big pine tree is growing near the road. The trail down the mountain starts just to the left of the tree. Think you can find your way down the mountain from the road?"

"I remember it," replied Phil. "We won't get lost if that's what you're worried about."

"I never felt that we really finished collecting there. Another full day ought to be about right. I'll let you off there by the tree and drive myself on down to the site we worked yesterday. Must be nearly a mile farther down the road."

"How will we know when to quit?" asked Phil.

"Let's just say we'll work till noon," replied Janice. "It will be too hot to work all day. I'll pick you up about an hour later if things are pretty normal. If the wind picks up too much before noon, climb back up the mountain and wait for me. The big pine tree will give you some shade. If I get back here before you are back up the mountain, I'll wait for you in the car."

"You won't wait in the car," said Phil. "It'll be too hot."

"I'll wait under the tree," said Janice.

After dropping Phil and Susan off, checking to see that they had all their equipment and warning them to be careful, Janice drove on to where she had parked the car yesterday. There was a level spot clear of chaparral. There was no shade, of course, but it was the only possible place to park. She opened the trunk and began to get her equipment together. Collecting net, two-quart canteen full of water, clipboard with tally sheets for keeping track of the kinds and numbers of insects caught or observed, and field notebook. Inside her backpack she checked for her first aid kit, vials full of alcohol for preserving soft bodied insects, snakebite kit, two cyanide insect-killing jars, various small empty bottles and tins to hold hard bodied insects, a Swiss army knife, hand lens, extra pencils, mouth aspirator for collecting tiny insects, aluminum-cloth protective blanket, some safety matches, and a few other odds and ends. Everything appeared to be there. She often wondered if she carried more than she had to, but most everything was either necessary or light in weight and might become indispensable in an emergency. The first aid kit was a little bulky and so was the aluminum-cloth blanket. However, the first might be vital in an emergency and the second would be needed if for any reason she was stuck out in the field overnight and had to keep her body warm.

After carefully replacing everything in her pack, she strapped it shut. Then she sat down on a rock and put on her snake guards. Janice was ready to start down the slope, but wanted desperately to have a cigarette first. She quickly debated with herself about it. Should she, on the one hand, take the time for something so unnecessary, and did she really have to self-indulge to this extent. On the other hand, what was five minutes more or less out of half a day, and maybe everyone needed a little self-indulgence.

Before losing this thought, she got into the car, opened the glove compartment, took a cigarette from the half-full pack and lit it with the car cigarette lighter.

The smell of the smoke blended with that of the chaparral. The chaparral always smelled good early in the morning. Spring, of course, was the best time of year because so many plants were blooming then, and the scent of nectar was heavy in the air. But even at the end of summer, one could enjoy some delicate fragrances. Janice could pick out the rather sharp penetrating odor of yerba santa, a leathery leafed shrub that was common on the brushy slopes of Southern California. It wasn't blooming now, but the leaves were aromatic throughout the year.

She wondered vaguely why so few entomologists were interested in chaparral insects. Certainly there was plenty of work to be done. Very little was known about the ecology of insects found in chaparral. One question she had was what happens to the insect populations after a fire when most of the shrubby plants are displaced for several years by herbaceous plants? Other workers had shown that initially the number and variety of insects change greatly. Where do these insects come from and where do they eventually go?

She suspected that many scientists avoided chaparral because they were reluctant to work under such adverse conditions. Every step was a challenge when the brush was especially thick. It was much more fun to work in the open forest, or almost anywhere else for that matter.

It was time to start down to the collecting area. Janice inhaled deeply from what was left of her cigarette and crushed it out in the ash tray below the dashboard. As she was getting out of the car, one snake guard caught on the edge of the door and almost tripped her.

"Bastard," she said softly to the door.

She gazed out over the valley below her. The air was still clear. There would be no smog today if the winds developed. It was beautiful. The great bulk of Mount San Jacinto stood out clearly to the east near Palm Springs. Closer and slightly to the north was San Gorgonio. To the south were the Santa Ana Mountains and to the west, out of her view, was Los Angeles. Below she could barely make out a couple of thin lines that she knew were freeways. They would be bumper to bumper with automobiles taking their owners to work and trucks taking their produce to market. It was commuting hour. The traffic would be barely crawling in most spots, or perhaps even gridlocked. There would be several accidents already out there, perhaps several people hurt or even killed. She shook her head at the absurdity of it all. How can they stand living like a bunch of trapped animals on the freeways, she thought to herself, being herded back and forth for several hours every day. Each day the same thing all over again. Those poor idiots! She gloried that she was free in the mountains. Then she lowered her eyes to the ground and started carefully down the steep slope.

SIX

For Susan and Phil the hike down wasn't too bad, although they had found that hiking downhill in thick chaparral was about as difficult as going uphill. It just didn't take as long because rest stops weren't necessary. They reached the general area where they had decided to start collecting in about 35 minutes. It would take the better part of an hour to get back up the hill.

"Rest a bit before we start?" suggested Phil.

"What? Are you kidding? Is the big man tired already?" taunted Susan.

"Yeah, I'm worn out. And I wanted to talk to you about us," said Phil seriously.

"I don't think this is the place or the time to discuss us," responded Susan. "I think we're supposed to be working, or do

I have it all wrong?" Susan tried to sound grim, but Phil could see a twinkle in her brown eyes.

"Well," said Phil," I wanted to talk to you about your parents a little bit. How tough do you think they are going to be? We had better start facing some of the serious problems instead of just telling each other how much in love we are. Your folks scare the hell out of me and I haven't even met them yet. What do they look like? Do they breathe fire? Why am I so scared?"

Susan laughed. "They look pretty human, but they eat white boys for lunch. Don't even bother to cook 'em, just eat 'em raw. Is there any way we could slant your eyes and darken your skin a little? And, my God, your red hair! We'll have to shave your whole body so they can't see what color your hair is. Maybe we can fix you up so you'll be more acceptable."

"Come on, Sue, I'm serious. I really am worried." Phil had a nervous tic that occasionally bothered him. He would roll his eyes upward and to the right. He did it when he was excited or worried. Susan noticed he was doing it now.

"Phil, I really don't think we should get into this right now. Let's collect some bugs. That's what we're supposed to be doing."

Phil sighed. "I'd rather make love if I had a choice."

Susan giggled. "Yes, I know, but Japanese-American girls don't make love in the chaparral. We're not allowed to."

"White boys like to and we get special instructions at the age of 14 on 25 different ways of screwing white girls in chaparral. It's one of the big things we look forward to when we're growing up.

Susan smirked. "Japanese-American girls are so good there's no need for 25 ways. Two or three are enough."

Phil suddenly put his hands on the sides of her face, tilted her head back and kissed her lips. "How about tonight?" he asked. "I need you."

"We'll see later," she said, gently pushing him away. But there was love showing in her eyes.

"Japanese-American girl will see rater if white boy can

prease her tonight," said Phil in his best rendition of a Japanese accent. "White boy must be patient until rater."

The breeze was beginning to pick up, swirling around the side of the mountain from the northeast. It was a very warm breeze, as if it had been trapped inside a hot oven and had just recently been liberated. It bent the few strands of brown, dry grass that stuck their heads up between the branches of the low lying brush. It swayed the tall brown sead-heads of California buckwheat plants growing here and there in the more open spots, agitating their small, hairy leaves with the margins characteristically turned under. It even stirred the chamise with its tiny, needle like leaves that were the wrong shape to catch the wind. Chamise, the plant found so abundantly in chaparral, and so dangerous because of its flammability.

They worked for some time in silence. Only the crunching of their boots on the rocky hillside and the swishing of their insect nets sweeping against the brush disturbed the stillness. Once in a while Susan would squeal with delight at some insect she had caught that was out of the ordinary. The breeze was picking up gradually and the insects were not abundant.

"Not good weather for collecting insects, Sue," said Phil. "What we need is a good rain and then a day or two after that, the insects would be out enjoying the humidity. The way it is now, they're sick of sunshine and dryness and heat. All they want to do is hide." Suddenly, he pulled his binoculars out of the case and focused on a couple of hawks doing acrobatics over the brush.

"I'm finding a few insects," replied Susan. "But I think it might be the breeze more than anything that is spooking them."

"Well, as long as we're here, we may as well do what we can I guess, said Phil.

"Why did you tell Dr. Ballard about us?" asked Susan. "I thought we agreed definitely not to tell anyone, Phil."

"Yeah, I know. It kind of slipped out, I guess. But I'm just as happy that she knows we're serious. She must have been having suspicions about us. After all, we used to work pretty much by ourselves and lately we've been working together constantly. She must have noticed. Anyway, she won't blab our secret around. I like Dr. Ballard. She's got a lot of good sense and she's certainly not gossipy. She won't tell anyone."

"No, I guess not," agreed Susan. "But it was sort of fun having it our own secret. Now it's not ours anymore."

"Well, I just didn't want Dr. Ballard to think we were goofing off."

"We could still be goofing off for all she knows," suggested Susan.

"It's not the same. She knows now that we're serious and we have our futures to think about."

"Anything you say, lover boy," said Susan, smiling at him and shaking the contents of her insect net into the killing jar.

"Would you like to go to school at Berkeley?" asked Phil.

"Well, it might be one of my choices if I have an opportunity. It certainly has one of the best entomology graduate departments in the country, if I decide to stay in entomology. And it's close. But there are other good schools not too far away," replied Susan. "But let's wait and see what happens. We have to see what you are going to do first. We have plenty of time to decide."

Once again they worked in silence, each glad for the presence of the other. The wind was blowing slightly harder now. It was a little after 10:00 by Phil's watch. The wind was parchingly dry and both Susan and Phil we're drinking liberally from their canteens.

"Gee, I'm glad we don't have to work all day," said Susan. "My canteen may be about dry by noon. This heat and wind is a bitch."

"I don't think there is any use trying to hold out much longer," replied Phil. "If the wind keeps getting stronger, I think we should go back up. Can't accomplish anything under these conditions. We probably never should have come out today."

Suddenly, Susan's hat blew off and Phil just missed grabbing it as it sailed past him.

"Do I have to chase after that thing?" asked Phil, grinning.

"You do if your a gentleman," replied Susan.

"I've never said I was a gentleman."

The hat had become stuck in the branches of a tall bush about 30 yards from Phil. Resigningly, he put down his pack and net and started for it.

"You should have got a hat with a chin strap like mine," hollered Phil against the wind. "Just proves that men are smarter than women."

They worked their way around the hill to the southwest side, which was more protected. Here the wind was not nearly as strong and they found the collecting was easier.

"We should have come around on this side earlier," observed Susan.

"Yeah, it would have been better," replied Phil.

They worked until 11:55 and started back up the side of the mountain. The wind seemed a little calmer now, as if it might be abating somewhat. But, it was extremely hot for the time of day. They took one extra rest stop going back up, but their sweaty clothes were clinging to them when they reached the road. Janice had had time to smoke a cigarette in the car and was waiting for them under the tree, eating her lunch.

Phil looked at her and said, "I'll bet you've been sitting under that tree all morning. How do we know you've been working?"

"You don't, but it would be my prerogative to sit here all day if I wanted to since I'm the boss," replied Janice, winking at Susan. "Anyway, you saw me driving away this morning before you started down."

"You could have come back 15 minutes later," replied Phil.

Janice wet her finger and held it up in the air as if to test the wind. "I think the wind has steadied," she said. "But we'll quit anyway because of the heat. I hope, if the wind cooperates, we can come back tomorrow and get in another half-day. Then we'll be done here in this spot."

After lunch, Phil and Susan climbed into Janice's car after

putting all their gear in the trunk. "Well, I can start entering some of the data we've collected into the computer this afternoon," declared Janice, "and I can get home a little earlier than usual. Hey, I've got a great idea. Why don't you two come over for steaks this evening. Tony Rogers will be there too. He and my son are getting home from the beach about dinner time. We could have a good visit, unless you have something else to do."

Susan and Phil looked at each other. Phil was hoping to do some lovemaking that evening, but it was hard to pass up a good steak. "Okay by me," he said.

"Great," added Susan. "I'm tired of my own cooking."

"We'll see you about seven then," said Janice.

Phil was in the shower. Susan had already taken hers. Phil had connived some ridiculous excuse to come back to Susan's apartment with her after they had come down off the mountain. It was obvious what was going to happen and they were both excited. Phil had no change of clothing, but he said he wouldn't need clothes for what he had in mind. He would go home and change clothes later.

Susan had turned on the window air conditioner and the apartment was a little less stifling than when they had arrived. She gathered three blankets from the closet and folded them in the shape of a narrow double bed. These were laid on the floor in the breeze of the air conditioner. Then she covered the blankets with a sheet. Everything was ready. She took off her robe and stretched out.

About ten minutes later, Susan decided that Phil was stalling. She laughed to herself about it. The shower had just now been turned off, and she guessed it would be at least five more minutes before Phil would appear, probably with a towel wrapped around his middle in an apparent show of modesty. This stalling procedure had occurred before, and she had decided that he was determined not to be perceived as coming on like some kind of animal. He wanted to let her know that he could restrain his desire, at least for a few minutes.

She decided to have some fun. "Hurry, Phil, I can't wait any longer," she called, laughing to herself.

"What did you say?" Phil stuck his head out the bathroom door. He had the most curious look on his face, as though he couldn't believe what he thought he had heard. He was still drying himself. He took one look at her naked body, dropped the towel and hurried out of the bathroom. There were still streaks of water on his chest and stomach. "You little devil," he said as she held her arms out to him. She was grinning broadly.

"This will be one you won't forget," he said softly.

"I won't forget any of them," she answered.

He buried his face in her stomach and kissed his way downward. In a few minutes when her hips were beginning to roll, he crawled up beside her and groaned with pleasure as it slipped inside.

SEVEN

The steaks were setting on the counter top next to the kitchen sink. Janice was busy making a second salad. She had planned only potato salad, but with Susan and Phil coming for dinner, a fruit salad would also be needed.

Tony and Todd had arrived back from the beach forty-five minutes ago. Tony had gone home to clean up. Janice could hear Todd's shower still running. It was hard to get him out of the shower once he was in.

The cat was banging at the back door waiting to be fed. It was a trick he had learned while still very young. He would put his front paws up on the screen door, stick his claws into the screen, and then shake. The banging noise could be heard all through the house. Jennifer was supposed to respond since it was her cat. But so far, Jennifer had not appeared.

"Darn that kid," Janice said to herself. "Jennifer, the cat wants some food! Are you deaf?" yelled Janice to the rest of the house. She wasn't sure where Jennifer was.

"Let him in, Mom. I'll feed him in a minute," came the reply from somewhere that sounded far away.

Sighing, Janice walked over and opened the screen door. The cat came in eagerly, holding its tail high and sniffing. "Can you smell that meat, Mickey? Jennifer will be here in a minute to get you something."

The cat was about two years old and made a perfect pet for Jennifer. She had gotten Mickey when he was still a baby. One of the neighbor's cats had had a litter of five, two males and three females. Mickey was sort of a strange color, a combination of orange and gray. Janice thought he was ugly at first and would have picked another one, probably one of the females. But she had become used to his looks and Jennifer delighted in him. He was cuddly, unlike some cats that can be standoffish. And he was a talker. Anyone giving him any attention whatever would be entertained by an uninterrupted series of long, mournful yowls, as if he had an unending list of complaints. He was a funny, lovable cat and he almost never scratched.

Jennifer suddenly appeared and scooped Mickey up in her arms. "Are you hungry, kitty?" she asked. Mickey responded with a nonstop wail that sounded a little like a bagpipe.

"Yes, dis kitty-cat is just starving to death. Nobody pays any 'tension to him," murmured Jennifer in a dubious rendition of baby talk. "Jenny will give you some food because she loves you." She got a can of food from the cupboard and opened it. The cat danced around her feet wailing miserably.

"Can he eat in here, Mom?" asked Jennifer.

"No, take him outside. His dish is by the back door. There's too much activity in the kitchen right now to have a cat underfoot," declared Janice.

The shower had finally stopped. Janice went over to the hall entrance and called to her son.

"Todd, when you get dressed, get the barbecue out of the

garage, please. Clean it off a little and get it ready to light." It was a gas barbecue and would take only a couple of minutes to heat up when everyone arrived.

"Okay, Mom," answered Todd. "Be ready in a minute."

Janice had earlier put a couple of bottles of white zinfandel in the refrigerator. She and Tony would have wine. She had also bought a six-pack of beer, not knowing whether Susan and Phil would prefer that to wine. She never kept beer in her home as a rule. She had never acquired a taste for it and preferred that it was not available to tempt the kids. She had seen too much abuse of beer by high school and college students. She had even seen younger children around the neighborhood, children that could not have been old enough to be in high school, drinking out of beer cans. The sight disgusted her.

Everything seemed to be about ready and she could sit down for a minute and read the *L. A. Times*. The headlines indicated that one out of every seven people in Los Angeles County was on welfare. "Great," said Janice to herself. "Just what we need."

A car door slammed out in front of the house. Janice got up and went to investigate. Phil and Susan had arrived. Phil was carrying a bottle of wine with him. Perhaps the beer would be unnecessary.

"You didn't have to bring anything," protested Janice. "Susan and I pooled our resources." replied Phil. "It's not the most expensive wine by any means. But, it's better than showing up empty handed." He handed Janice the bottle, grinning at her.

"Come on in," said Janice. "Tony should be back shortly and then we can start the steaks. Let's go out in back where it's a little cooler than in the house." Susan and Phil had been to Janice's house once before to discuss the chaparral research project, so they had met the children and the cat.

Five minutes later another car door slammed out front announcing the arrival of Tony.

"Anybody home?" he called from the front door.

"Come on through, Tony," yelled Janice from the kitchen. "Phil is putting the steaks on the grill."

"Wow, that was good, Dr. Ballard!" exclaimed Phil. "I haven't eaten potato salad that good in ages. I'd marry anybody who can make potato salad like that."

"Thanks anyway, but I'm too old for you, Phil," laughed Janice. Besides, I'm not sure that Su—." Janice had almost said too much. She had nearly exposed the secret. "I mean, I think you would get tired of potato salad three times a day. It's almost all I know how to make."

"That really was good, Janice," added Tony. Apparently he was not aware of the near slip. "You have any objection to an older man?"

"Is that a proposal?" asked Janice, smiling. "If it is, I accept."

"I was thinking more in general than personal terms," said Tony with a slightly embarrassed grin on his face. Janice laughed but felt a little embarrassed too, with a tinge of emptiness deep down inside.

Jennifer and Todd had disappeared. Probably they had gone to watch television or to do something which they considered more interesting than listening to after dinner grownup talk. Janice and Susan began clearing the dishes.

They had to be carried from the outside patio, where dinner had been eaten, into the kitchen. There they would go into the dishwasher. To Janice's surprise, both of the men began helping with the carrying.

"You guys don't need to help," said Janice. "This won't take long."

"No one will ever call me lazy," said Phil. "Besides, it's the least I can do after that great meal."

Tony said nothing, but that was not unusual for him. He was a quiet and thoughtful man. Janice had wondered whether he preferred the quietness and uncomplicated life of bachelorhood. Perhaps that was why he had never married. Certainly, he was not unattractive. Well over six feet tall and with a lean, but well-muscled body. He had serious brown eyes that had attracted Janice from the very first time she had seen him. They gave him a look of trustworthiness. Here was a man that could be counted on. He would not let you down when things got tough. His fawn colored hair was beginning to recede ever so slightly above his forehead. Someday he would be mostly bald, but still attractive. His ears were shaped perfectly in Janice's estimation.

She had always considered her own ears as being too large, and she covered them by wearing her hair over them. It was thick hair, chestnut brown in color, like her mother's had been at one time. She also had her mother's build, small boned but not skinny, and medium height.

She had her dad's strong jaw, straight nose, and dark blue eyes. She was one of those women who was nothing special at first glance, but whose beauty grew the more you looked at her. Jennifer would probably look much like Janice someday, whereas Todd was beginning to take on some of the physical characteristics of his father.

The dishwasher was making a muffled roaring noise. Phil, who had insisted on washing the pots and pans and whatever else would not fit into the dishwasher, was nearly finished. He had stacked the various utensils in the drainer in such a way that there was serious danger of an accident. A slight jar and the entire pile would go. Janice had brought out the six-pack of beer, hoping that someone would drink at least part of it. She would send the rest home with one of them.

It was beginning to cool off a little now. Even the inside of the house was starting to feel better. The house was not air conditioned, so she and the kids just had to suffer through the hot spells that came frequently at the end of summer. Todd often slept on the patio when the nights were warm. At least the humidity was usually pretty low.

All four of them selected lawn folding-chairs and pulled them up into a circle on the patio. Tony and Phil decided to top off their dinner with a glass of cold beer. Susan said she wasn't much of a beer drinker.

"So, what are your plans, Phil?" inquired Tony. "Are you leaving us pretty soon? Is your thesis finished?"

Phil groaned. "I wish I could say it was finished and there was a good job waiting for me," he replied. "But I haven't even begun it yet. I don't much enjoy writing. The fun part is doing the field work."

Tony smiled. "I guess everybody feels pretty much the same way about that," he said. "How about it, Janice? Do you like to write up your data after the field work is finished?"

"Hate it," replied Janice. "Maybe some day there will be computers that you can feed sheets of raw data into and they will write a paper for you. I'd buy one of those if I could afford it."

"I don't mind writing," said Susan. "I sort of enjoy it. It is like an ego trip. You can say anything you want to. You're in charge."

"Not in a scientific paper," exclaimed Phil. "You gotta say what the data tells you to say!"

"Well, sure, I mean you can say it in your own way," replied Susan.

"You haven't written a thesis yet," said Phil. "Maybe you'll change your mind."

"I've written plenty of reports," said Susan. "They can't be that much different."

Tony and Janice glanced at each other. "Let's not fight about it, kids," said Janice. "This is supposed to be a quiet and peaceful party."

"Any jobs out there?" inquired Tony of Phil.

"No," replied Phil. "Very few. The economy is supposed to be getting better, but there aren't any jobs out there like I need. The state government is broke, the federal government is broke, the counties and cities are broke. Many businesses are trying to economize, and I don't see much on the horizon. Seems like we've been waiting for an economic recovery that is slow in happening in Southern California. The economists keep predicting better times."

"I sure don't believe anything the economists say," said

Janice. "They don't have the faintest idea what the future will bring. Talk about a pseudo science! Economics has got to be the biggest joke in town."

"Economists just don't have a solid basis to predict from," said Tony. "There are too many variables, all working independently at any one time. Who can tell what will happen when even such things as the mood of the people and how they react is important. But I'm not too worried about the economic situation. It'll recover eventually. It always does. I'm worried about other things. Our whole social structure seems to be failing. I've been watching it for a while. No one trusts anyone anymore. Politicians are fakers or worse. Some are outright criminals. Lawyers seem to be in business for the money; forget about justice. Is there anybody out there that will tell the truth and act with some integrity? I don't know."

These latter comments were a big surprise for Janice. She had never experienced this side of Tony before. Previously, whenever they had talked, he had appeared to be calm and pretty optimistic about everything. Perhaps even good old Tony was getting the message. Sometimes she wondered whether she was too negative about things. But she had always been a cautious person, and it seemed to her that there were more and more problems in modern society that were not being addressed properly. Perhaps some were beyond a reasonable remedy already.

"People call me a worrier, I suppose," said Janice. "But I see things I don't like too. I see more students who think cheating is acceptable. Lying creates no guilt or even embarrassment."

"But what can you expect, Dr. Ballard?" added Susan. "This is what we experience every day. Our government leaders, our heroes, our idols, the media. Everyone lies and cheats. They lie to get elected, or to get out of trouble, or to get rich, or to get ahead. They lie and cheat because its acceptable. It's either forgiven or forgotten, even if they get caught."

"Yeah," put in Phil. "It sure makes it easier to understand a student's dishonesty."

"The disturbing thing to me is the lack of guilt," said Tony. "Morality and ethics for their own sake seem to be extinct. But I wonder sometimes if it's still out there in many people and we just don't see it because our attention is diverted. The news media doesn't make a big thing out of people's honesty most of the time. The rotten things people do seem to be more newsworthy than the good things. The media follows disreputable celebrities around like rats following the Pied Piper. Doesn't give you a whole lot of respect for the media."

"You know what my dad thinks is one of the most unethical examples of behavior?" said Susan. "Most people don't think much about it apparently. It's the way famous athletes, entertainers and other well-known people accept money from industry to endorse a product. These people are often making millions each year by acting in front of lights or bouncing basketballs around a court, but they make even more by wearing a brand label or giving testimony as to how good a product is. Dad calls them prostitutes. He says most of them couldn't care less about the product. They're prostituting themselves just for the money."

"Yeah, and almost all of them do it," put in Phil. "Our sports heroes and entertainers are a bunch of prostitutes! That's pretty funny. I never thought about it that way before. But it's common practice even among university and college athletic departments. The better known basketball teams, for example, accept free shoes for their players from the manufacturers. Of course, the little known teams have to buy their own shoes. Some of the top coaches get hundreds of thousands of dollars in kickbacks from the manufacturers for making their athletes wear a certain brand. And it's all legal. I wonder what would happen if a biology professor at a big university tried something like that. He'd be looking for a new job the next day. The latest trend is for entire universities to get kickbacks. They're beginning to make contracts worth millions of dollars."

"Speaking of ethics in sports," said Tony, "there's one

thing that used to bug my folks about sports fans. I guess they thought of it as dishonesty. I just thought it was amusing. It's the way many fans identify themselves with a winning team. It's as if they themselves had something to do with the team's success. If the team is not successful, then, of course, they want nothing to do with it. Mom, especially, used to get real upset. She'd say, 'If you can't be loyal to a team when its losing as well as winning, then you have no business being a sports fan'. Of course, sports are a bigger deal in the Middle West than they are here."

"But aren't a lot of those people just losers in general?" asked Janice. "I mean many of them have had no success in their own personal lives. The only success they are ever going to have is taking someone else's and making it their own. That's kind of sad."

"Some of them probably are losers," replied Tony. "But I've seen highly respected people act this way too. Some people are sports crazy anyway. Maybe they have nothing else to think about."

"Well, I wish that was the worst of it," said Janice. "That's pretty mild stuff. I'm concerned about more serious things. Look at the Rodney King incident. People just waiting for some excuse to burn and loot. Most of those looters in L. A. couldn't have cared less about Rodney King. It was a circus atmosphere. They just wanted to raise hell and get what they could by stealing."

"Yeah, and whole families were doing it," added Phil. "Little kids were along with their parents looting stores. Those people acted more like animals than humans. Taking their kids out where they could get killed. There were people with guns out there! What the hell is wrong with those idiots? By the way, didn't they used to shoot looters?"

"Isn't greed what it's all about?" suggested Janice. "Isn't everybody just getting greedy, from the top level all the way down? We seem to have lost our perspective of what life is all about. The benefits and gratification of hard work. The ideal of sacrificing now so the future can be better. All of the things this country once believed in seem to have disappeared. Everybody wants instant gratification."

"I don't think its as simple as just greed," said Tony. "I think its more complex. Greed is certainly a part of it. But ignorance and irresponsibility are also a part of it. Many people and institutions ignore the problems. People don't want to read to educate themselves, or maybe they never learned how to read. Others are just complacent. It's easier to sit in front of a television set and watch dumb programs and even dumber commercials. Still others are irresponsible. They don't want to take care of their kids or their debts, and they don't care about the rights of others. Some refuse to be open minded. Look at many of the religious fundamentalists that refuse to recognize scientific evidence for what it is. Look at the Creationists that live in a make-believe world. Look at the Roman Catholic Church that can't seem to escape from the seventeenth century. Its refusal to admit that its policies on birth control are having deleterious implications for the earth's overcrowded future is absurd. I could think of other things if I had time."

"The most insidious trend I've seen over the past few years is the killing of people by other people for no reason," said Janice. "It used to be that they killed for money or drugs. Now it's just to kill! No reason necessary. It's even happening among children. Kids kill other kids needlessly and there's no remorse. Of course, some of it is drug or gang related. It's happening not far from here. Gang members shooting other gang members. It makes me wonder how safe my own kids are."

"Don't you think some of that is because of the needless violence kids see on television and at the movies?" suggested Susan. "Television and movies are saturated with violence. The kids become blasé about it. My folks won't even go to the movies anymore. They say most of them are garbage. The unnecessary bad language, sex and violence seems to be too much for them. I think the last movie they saw was *Driving Miss Daisy*. They liked that one because it didn't have any of the bad elements and it had a point to make. Television is just as bad. Try to find anything on commercial television with a point to it."

"You live in a mostly Latino area here, don't you, Dr. Ballard? Does that present any problems?" asked Phil.

"It's predominately Latino now," answered Janice. "I like most of my neighbors, but there's also the gang element. I'm beginning to worry about it."

"Have you had any shootings in your neighborhood?" asked Phil.

"About two blocks away," replied Janice. "And we hear what are probably shots sometimes."

"Wow!" exclaimed Susan. "I'm not sure I'd want to live around here."

"I'm not sure I want to either," replied Janice. "But here I am. Me and my two kids!" As she said it, Janice smiled wanly, as if to make light of it. But Tony had a different impression. She feels sort of trapped, he thought to himself.

"Maybe you should make an effort to move, Janice," said Tony.

"How can I move?" she replied. "It takes money to move to better areas. I'd probably like to live in Claremont or La Verne or San Dimas, where many of the faculty at the university live. But most of them are double income families. This house I live in would be worth 50,000 dollars more if it were situated in Claremont, only three or four miles away. I just can't afford to pay that much more for a house."

"Yes, I couldn't believe the difference in prices in various areas when I first came here," admitted Tony.

"Sometimes I feel like a poor relative," continued Janice. "I'm stuck down here in an area which is quickly becoming a barrio. Maybe it has some advantages, though. Maybe my kids will learn how to cope with kids who have different aspirations then they do. At the very least, they won't be expecting to go to the most expensive colleges like some of the Claremont kids." Janice grinned as she spoke. "Jennifer and Todd will have to survive on something less than the best."

"That won't necessarily hurt them," said Phil. "They'll survive all right, and they'll be all the tougher."

"As long as we're talking about problems," said Tony, "there are plenty of them at the university. Sometimes I wonder if we'll survive, Janice. Working for the state doesn't mean you're protected like many people think!"

"Oh, I don't know," replied Janice. "I suppose some of the faculty will survive even when there's nothing else left. When our equipment is finally all broken or too antiquated to use anymore, and when supplies are no longer available, I suppose we'll have to draw pictures on the blackboard to show the students how we used to teach."

"Providing you have any chalk," laughed Phil.

"Well, one thing is sure," said Tony, the university system is in real trouble unless somebody comes up with a way to finance it. If the state would rather build prisons than pay for higher education, who else is there besides the students? And are students going to be able to afford the cost?"

"But what can we do?" inquired Susan. "We have to have that education to get any kind of a decent job, even though right now those jobs are pretty scarce and the competition is fierce. We can't just quit school."

"I suppose not," agreed Tony. "Maybe industry and business will have to do their share. After all, they benefit from getting educated people to do their work for them, and they pay very little into the educational system presently." Complete silence followed as if every one had tired of the pessimistic vein of the conversation.

"Hey, can't we talk about something a little less depressing for a change?" suggested Phil.

It was a quarter to ten when Janice glanced at her watch. She looked at Phil and Susan. "What do you two want to do tomorrow?" she asked. "I haven't heard a weather forecast this evening. The wind seems to have pretty much stopped. Do you want to go back up on the mountain for half a day? We could probably finish the work in that particular area. Or, do you want to wait until next week? I'll leave it up to you."

Phil and Susan looked at each other. "I'd just as soon finish," said Phil. "How about it, Susan?"

"Yes, it's okay with me," she replied. "Then we can get a change of scenery next week."

"In that case I suggest we break up the party and get some sleep since the three of us will be getting up early. Is that okay with you, Tony? Or do you insist on keeping the party going?"

"It sounds to me like I'd be talking to myself, " Tony said smiling. "I guess that wouldn't be too much fun. I'll have to accept my fate graciously and go home too."

"It was just a great dinner, Dr. Ballard," said Phil. "I'll work extra hard tomorrow in appreciation."

"Yes, it was wonderful," added Susan. "Thank you so much for inviting us." She turned to Tony. "It was really nice talking to you, Dr. Rogers. We haven't seen you much this summer."

"Well, I've been dipping quite a bit in the ocean," replied Tony. "My work is at the beach."

"Must be a tough life, Tony," said Janice grinning sarcastically. "I wouldn't mind spending my summers at the beach and saying it was work!"

After the two students had left, Tony asked Janice if there was any more cleaning up he could help her with. "I don't think so," she said. "Everything is in good shape. But thank you for being considerate. What are you doing tomorrow, Tony?"

"Back to the computer, I guess. Have to do the drudgery stuff sometime."

They were out in front now by his car. "Thank you, Janice. It was a splendid evening. I get sort of lonesome sometimes, so I appreciate things like this."

"Anytime you get lonesome, come on over," said Janice. "As for the dinner, I still owe you a couple."

"You don't owe me anything," replied Tony. He was close to her now. Without warning he cupped her chin in his hand and kissed her. She was so surprised she almost didn't respond. Just as he was beginning to release her, she put both arms around his neck and returned the kiss.

"Goodnight," he said.

"Goodnight, Tony."

EIGHT

When Joe Agramonte came into the building, no one was at the front desk, but he could hear two voices back in the coffee area. One was Gloria's and the other belonged to Jason Kelly. It was a little after 8:00 A.M., September 14. Gloria had been working at the front desk for the past couple of years. She was extremely pretty and did her work satisfactorily. Kelly had been trying to get a date with her for several months. Unfortunately for him, she was totally uninterested.

Jason Kelly—everyone called him Jack, which seemed to fit him better—was one of those people who came off as being pretty sharp when you first met him. He always had a ready answer to everything. Only after you got to know him did it become apparent that he was a mimic. He probably had never had a single original thought in his life. He had memorized a considerable number of cute phrases that he had stolen from mindless TV situation comedies. Jack could apply these cuties with remarkable agility in almost any conversation as long as it did not get into a serious vein. He was completely lost when it came to serious dialogue, and he rigorously avoided conversations that had any substance to them. Kelly also mimed facial expressions and body language that he had seen on television and at movies. He was good at being a fake. Perhaps he was a genius.

Joe Agramonte disliked Kelly intensely, as did several others who knew him. Joe wasn't even sure exactly where Kelly worked or what he did at FIRESCOPE. Hopefully, his job wasn't very important. Probably he was just a flunky of some sort.

Agramonte worked for the U.S. Forest Service. He had been at FIRESCOPE for over five years. Before that he had been a field man in fire suppression with the Forest Service and he had enjoyed it immensely, especially when he was younger. But as he got older, it became more difficult physically to keep up, and Joe was overweight anyway.

So when he was offered a chance to go with FIRESCOPE, he decided to accept the opportunity. It would be a good place to retire from in a few years.

FIRESCOPE came into being as a result of the disastrous two week siege of fires throughout California in late September and early October, 1970. Nearly 700 structures and 16 lives had been lost. Congress had appropriated funding that resulted in a program that better coordinated federal, state, county and local fire suppression services. Most lacking was a centralized information center where up-to-the-minute data could be collected, processed and distributed to fire fighting units in fast changing fire situations region wide. This central information center for Southern California became FIRESCOPE and was located in Riverside.

The facility presently consisted of several buildings that were occupied by U. S. Forest Service personnel and those from several other cooperative agencies. The building where

Joe worked was inundated with computers, computer moni-tors, and data files. Entire walls were covered with such things as display maps where the location of fire fighting equipment and personnel could be kept track of and where weather information could be shown. The setup was rather impressive to visitors. Not only could fire fighting be coordinated here, but other kinds of disasters could be coordinated as well.

Joe was apprehensive about what the day might bring. Yesterday he had been gone most of the day to a meeting with some other "disaster freaks" as he called them. He had been concerned yesterday morning by the high atmospheric pres-sure area over the Great Basin and the developing low pres-sure off of Southern California. This would bring Santa Ana winds if that contrasting system kept developing, and that would cause problems for him. When he returned late in the afternoon, he checked the meteorological data as was his custom a couple of times a day. The pressure differences had stabilized between the two areas. This morning Joe was particularly anxious to check the data again. He was shocked by what he saw. The difference between the Great Basin high in Nevada and the low off Southern California was approach-ing 13 millibars of mercury, greater than he could ever remember. This would mean a very strong Santa Ana condi-tion developing today. The winds could be devastating.

"Hey, Al," he called to one of the men wearing a Forest Service uniform on the other side of the large room. "Have you seen this pressure difference?"

The man turned, peered over the rims of his glasses so he could recognize the speaker. "Hi, Joe. Yeah, I saw it. Scary huh?"

"Do you think it's correct?" inquired Joe.

"Well, I wondered about that too. So I checked with a couple of other people as soon as I could get them on the phone. Everybody's got the same reading. It's real all right. Get ready for some fun, Joe. Every goddamned arsonist in the county will be out there starting fires today."

Joe groaned to himself. Al was right. Not only in the

county, but probably all over Southern California. Not only arsonists, but power lines blown down by the wind, camp fires out of control, sparks from all kinds of sources. God only knew what the day would bring. With that thought he returned to his office and tried to concentrate on some of his routine daily tasks. He would stick around the office today and wait.

NINE

Janice looked at her watch. It was 8:31 A.M. She had left Phil and Susan by the large pine tree nearly two hours earlier. Then she had driven herself to the spot where she had parked yesterday, smoked one cigarette in the car, and trudged down the hill to her own collecting site.

It was even hotter today than yesterday at this time of the morning. The wind had begun to pick up too. Janice wished she had taken time to catch today's weather forecast. Were strong Santa Ana winds forecast for today? They hadn't developed yesterday until later on in the morning, and then they had sort of fizzled out by afternoon. She hoped they would do the same today.

Janice had seen a rattlesnake a few minutes before. She heard it long before she saw it. In fact, she heard it long before she thought it could be aware of her presence, as if something else had already disturbed it. It appeared highly upset when she finally spotted it about twenty feet ahead in an open spot. It was coiled, rattling its tail and darting its tongue out in several directions. This was the eighth encounter she had had with rattlesnakes in her chaparral work. She could remember each one distinctly. She had not become complacent about their presence, and she still felt frightened each time she came in contact with one. It would cause her to be more cautious of where she stepped for a few days until her composure was regained. Each snake seemed to have its own personality. Some were highly excitable and would rattle even before she was close enough to see them. Others would not make a sound until they were nearly stepped on. These were the ones she was particularly afraid of. Even the snake guards around her legs did not do much to relieve her anxiety. This particular snake had acted pretty weird. What was he doing out under these conditions? It was already blistering hot, and this snake was right out in the sun. Snakes usually don't like so much heat.

She regretted that her mind was not on her work today. She had been thinking all morning about Tony's kiss last night, and what it meant. Was he really interested in her, or was that just his way of thanking her for dinner? There was no way she could ask him. She would just have to wait and see what developed. But was he expecting some reaction from her? Sure, she had returned his kiss, but was that enough? Janice didn't really know how to handle the situation. If he was expecting some signal from her that he didn't get, he might decide she was not interested and feel rejected. She certainly didn't want that to happen. On the other hand, she didn't want to frighten him away with some stupid romantic gesture that he was not prepared for. She might even lose his friendship under these conditions. She would think about it some more, but right now the appropriate action appeared to be caution. She would let him make the advances and just hope that he would understand how she felt.

Janice worked on, lost in her thoughts. She vaguely

realized that the wind was rising rapidly. She wasn't too concerned, however, because the same thing had happened yesterday. It had become pretty strong before it started to die again. She would stay and see whether it would get calmer later on. And she felt that Phil and Susan would do the same thing since all of them had talked about it in the car coming up the mountain this morning. They were all anxious to stick it out and finish working the area today. Janice caught a movement out of the corner of her eye. It was a coyote running along the side of the mountain above her, seemingly unaware of her presence. This was really unusual. A coyote out this time of day? Perhaps the wind was spooking some of the animals. She could think of no other explanation for his being out running in this heat. Did something scare him? He seemed to be in a hurry. And the rattlesnake had acted funny too. Maybe this would just be one of those days when strange things were going to happen.

Janice glanced at her watch again. It was nearly 9:30. The wind was blowing hard now, and she decided to sit down in as much shade as she could find and rest a bit. It would also give the wind a chance to abate somewhat, if that was what it was going to do, even if it took an hour or more. She would just have to put up with being uncomfortable in the heat. After all, this was what research was all about. It wasn't always comfortable, but it was always exciting. No one had ever tried to do what she was doing. Her work was totally new and there was always the possibility of completely new insights. And even if there were to be no surprises, research was always gratifying for its own sake. She was the only person on earth, as far as she knew, who was doing this particular research. There was something thrilling about being the only one. She was unique.

The arsonist had been waiting patiently. Weeks ago he had made up his mind that he would not waste another opportunity. He would wait for the first strong Santa Ana, and then he would do it. It was no good procrastinating anymore. He had thought it out very carefully and had finally decided that it was the only way to show them. They had laughed at him and called him a loser, an underachiever, a drag on society, a parasite. Even his own family had no respect for him. His old man hadn't spoken to him in months. His weak mother would not even meet with him to talk once in a while. She was too frightened of what the old man might do if he found out. He had no friends any longer. One by one they had deserted him.

He had made his plans carefully. No one must be able to prove anything. He must be very careful. One fire would probably not be sufficient. Many fires might be necessary before these idiots could be taught to have proper respect for him. Perhaps some of his tormentors would even die if they were stupid enough to get near the fires. Served them right. His first fire must be a spectacular success, but he would keep building upon it. Each one would be more destructive and more memorable, and after each fire he would somehow inform them that he alone was responsible. They would learn that he was no failure. But he would be very sly and cryptic so that no one could be sure. Very cleverly he would let them know it was him, but they would never be able to prove anything. No loser could plan anything this devastating and cover his tracks so completely. They would learn to fear and respect the very thought of him. The stupid cops would look like fools. The fire fighters would be able to do nothing. He had always wanted to be a fire fighter, but they, too, had rejected him. Well, they would pay for that mistake. He would make each and every one of those sons of bitches pay, and pay dearly. His family, his would-be friends, the cops, the fire fighters. To hell with all of them.

He parked his car in a place he had carefully picked out earlier. It was hidden from the main road, yet he could observe the road in both directions to make sure no one saw him driving from the spot after the fire was set. He must move fast once the deed was done. The excitement was nearly over-whelming. This was the beginning of a new life for him. He had some highway flares in the back seat of his car, but was uncertain whether to take one with him. The brush was so dry it should start by just using matches. But the wind! Would the wind blow out the matches too quickly? He decided to take a flare with him just in case.

He planned to start the fire on the other side of the hill from the road, and down in a gully. That way the smoke would not be seen as quickly from the road. It would give him a chance to return to his car and make good his departure. Then a new thought struck him. He might even report the fire! God! Wouldn't that be something! He could drive to the fire station at the bottom of the mountain and report that he had seen smoke. By that time the fire would be too hot for them to handle in this wind. He was shaking with excitement as he worked his way around the hill, keeping out of sight of the road. There was no brush here and he could run back quickly the same way he had come when he was finished. The gully was just ahead. The wind was strong. Even during the last 20 minutes it had increased significantly. What a perfect setup!

He was at the gully now. There was a little more shelter from the wind here, but it was still gusting strongly. He decided against the matches; they would be too slow. Many would be blown out by the wind and it would take too long. Besides, his hands were shaking so violently he wasn't sure he could handle matches easily. He looked at the flare in his hand. Then he took a long, careful look all around. He saw nothing disturbing. There was only the chaparral moving in the wind. He listened. But there was no chance of hearing anything unusual. The wind was making too much noise. He was dripping with sweat. He needed to urinate, but there was no time now. He carefully ignited the flare. Then he worked quickly starting a line of fire at right angles to the wind. He was surprised how quickly the brush flamed up. Maybe he could have used matches after all. After he had lit perhaps 30 feet of brush, he threw the flare as far as he could in the direction the fire was burning. The flare would burn completely and would leave no trace of how the fire started. He glanced back at the line of fire. There was too much smoke and it scared him.

He was running now, back the way he had come. He wanted to look back, but he didn't. He was completely winded when he reached the car, got in, looked carefully up and down the road. There were no cars in sight. He was almost finished now. He drove onto the road and looked for smoke, but he could see nothing. It had worked out perfectly. His planning had paid off. Now he could relax. His hands were still shaking a little, but they were better. It wouldn't be long now and he would be off the mountain and home free. Just like playing hide-and-seek when he was a kid. It would feel good to be "home free."

He drove for several minutes. He was exhilarated. He could hardly wait to get to the bottom of the mountain. The fire should be really moving by now. Maybe he could see the smoke if he looked back. Then suddenly his car was out of control. He swore to himself. The steering was gone. The car veered crazily from one side of the road to the other. The road seemed to be moving; it was rolling almost like waves on water! What the hell was going on? He could hold the car no longer. It swerved one final time and dove over the edge of the embankment. There was a sheer drop. The car did more than a full turn in the air before impacting with a giant rock sticking out from the cliff. The arsonist had not bothered to fasten his seat belt. His head smashed through the driver's-side window. Then the door released and he plunged on down the cliff. Somehow the car remained wedged between the rock and the embankment, two of its wheels spinning slowly.

TEN

"This wind is getting awfully strong, Susan," said Phil. "It's worse than yesterday."

"What time does your watch say?" asked Susan.

"It's just about twenty to ten."

"Well, I think we ought to stick it out a while," said Susan. "That's what we all agreed on in the car before Dr. Ballard dropped us off. Remember?"

"Yeah, I remember," said Phil wearily. "But I think it's time for a break anyway. See any shade anywhere?"

"Uh—there might be a little under that scrub oak over there. Just enough for one person. You can find your own shade."

"We could cuddle," he suggested grinning.

"Not in this heat we couldn't."

Somehow they both managed to sprawl in the scanty shade provided by the shrub. While Phil untied his boots, Susan removed her hat and took a long drink of water. If the wind got any worse she would have to carry her hat, or put it in her pack. Phil was right, she should have bought one with a chin strap. The wind was from the northeast, but here on the south side of the mountains there were eddies that were blowing in crazy directions. Susan looked out over the valley. The air was not as clear as it had been earlier. Certainly it couldn't be smog with all this wind, she thought. It must be dust. The wind is strong enough to start blowing dust through the valley. This may be the end of our collecting insects for today.

Phil had his boots off now and his shirt unbuttoned down the front. He put his head on his pack and closed his eyes.

"Wake me when the wind dies down, Susan. I'm still a growing boy and I need all the sleep I can get."

"Sometimes these things blow for three or four days, you know," she said.

"Good, then I'll sleep for three or four days."

The wind made Susan sleepy also in spite of the heat. She closed her eyes and began to daydream about her childhood. She and her sister had been very close. Patty was two years younger than she. They had had some great times together. Susan had been sort of a mother to Patty, watching over her at the beach to make sure she didn't get caught in the undertow, making sure that she was okay when they were at camp in the mountains. Patty was smart like Susan. Probably even smarter. But her tastes were different. Patty had always liked people, and people were attracted to her. Part of it may have been because Patty was so pretty. She didn't have the squarish face that Susan had inherited from her father. Patty's face was more round like her mother's and her laughing, dark eyes expressed her personality. Patty was not particularly interested in animals or plants the way Susan was. She had entered UCLA as a pre-med student two years ago. Patty would make a great physician, Susan thought to herself. Susan's brother, Larry, was five years older than she, and she wished that she knew him better. Perhaps there was too much of an age gap. Larry was an engineer and worked for a corporation in Sunnyvale. Susan's family was closely knit and secure. Everyone supported one another when the need arose.

Phil's family was very different. Susan had had a difficult time getting Phil to talk about his family, but one evening when they had drunk a little more wine than usual, he finally loosened up. His father was something of a drifter and part-time alcoholic. He had been able to find jobs here and there, mostly far away from home. The six kids rarely saw him, but he was good about sending his family a little money now and then. On the rare occasions when he did come home he usually left Phil's mother pregnant. Phil was second to the oldest child. His older sister was nearly as much in charge of the family as his mother. As Phil got older he began to realize what a burden his sister had, and he began feeling sorry for her and helped her as much as possible. But she never complained and apparently loved all the kids as they appeared, one by one. His mother also loved them, but she had to work to make a living and was content to let her oldest daughter keep the household organized. They lived in a three-room building that had once been a very small church. The congregation had long since disbanded. All the kids slept out in the big room that had been the church sanctuary. It also served as a kitchen, dining room and living room.

Of course, there was no money for college, but Phil was intelligent and had been influenced by one of his high school instructors to try to find some way to attend. Part-time jobs had kept him going in a two year community college and subsequently at the university. It took him five years to graduate because he had to work so many hours. Susan was impressed by what Phil had accomplished on his own. He was really a nice guy with a big heart. He was absolutely honest and there was not a phony bone in his body. His personality was open and frank; there had been no time nor opportunity to develop any frills. She was very much in love with him. It was the first time she had felt this way. She had not been interested in boys in high school, and had dated only two or three times in college.

Whether Susan's parents would readily accept Phil, however, was of some concern to her. Her brother had married a Japanese-American girl, so there had been no problem there. She suspected her parents would be upset, but would probably adjust eventually. They were pretty reasonable people and would come to love and respect him as soon as they saw how she felt about him. Things would work out. She would make them work out.

Phil had gone to sleep. Susan could hear his heavy breathing above the noise of the wind. She turned to get more comfortable and was dropping off to sleep when the earth seemed to fall out from under her. For an instant she thought that it must be a terrifying dream. But then she knew it was no dream and the earth really was moving violently. It seemed to be undulating. There had been one spastic jolt and a terrifying roar from the guts of the earth, and now the ground was rolling like waves on the ocean. She realized with a sick feeling in her stomach that it was a severe earthquake. She tried to stand but couldn't. Phil seemed to be still half-asleep. He was sitting up now but looked completely dazed and unable to comprehend what was happening.

"Phil," she screamed. "It's an earthquake. What shall we do?"

Phil was alert now and grabbed her hand. "We'll wait until it's over," he yelled. She could barely hear him in the noise of the wind and the rumble of the earth's moving, but the look in his eyes gave her confidence. Together they would wait it out. The rolling seemed to go on and on as if it would never stop. Dust was everywhere. Rocks were rolling down the slope. Susan wondered if they could be caught in a landslide. Finally, with one last grinding groan, the earth stopped moving and it was quiet again except for the wind and the sound of a few tumbling rocks still trying to find a place to rest.

"That wasn't so bad was it, Susan?"

She stared at Phil. He had almost a comical look of uncertainty on his face as he said it. She could have laughed if she hadn't been so scared. She thought to herself that he must be having a hard time believing his own words.

"Are you crazy?" she replied. "That was really bad! That must have been the big one everyone has been waiting for." She was shaking and wasn't sure she could stand up.

He helped her to her feet and they held each other for a long moment. Then he sat down again and began putting on his boots. "I wonder how Dr. Ballard is," he said. "We had better go back up the hill and see if we can find her. We can walk down the road to where she parked her car in case she's not at the big pine tree where she left us this morning."

They started off up the hill. Suddenly Susan stopped dead still. "Do you smell smoke?" she asked.

Phil sniffed the air. "Yeah," he said.

"My God, don't tell me the chaparral is on fire!"

Janice had been resting 20 minutes or more. She had lost track of the time. Her body was hot and sweaty and her mind was still preoccupied with thoughts of Tony and last night. She felt confused and indecisive. Was she in love with Tony? Did she know him well enough to be in love with him? Or did she just need someone to be close to and to share with, and Tony happened to be available. But even more questionable, was Tony in love with her? She was probably just being silly. One kiss doesn't mean much. Hell, what does anything mean anymore? Nowadays people routinely bed down with other people and even *that* is no commitment. Perhaps Tony was just feeling lonely. Yes, that was it. Probably nothing more was intended. He wasn't the marrying type like she was. At one time she had wondered if he were gay. But as she came to know him better she refused to believe it. Now she needed to know him better before she let herself fall very deeply in love with him. And much more important still, she needed to know exactly how he felt about her. That would probably be difficult to find out.

She roused herself from her reverie. The wind was blowing harder than ever. What to do? Give up working for the day and go back to the car? But she had asked Susan and Phil to stick it out for a while even if the wind did continue. They would probably not come back up to the road until noon no matter what the wind did. It was too windy to collect insects. But maybe she could find a better spot with more shade where she could sit and wait. Either that or she could climb back up to the car and drive back to the big pine, where the two students would appear sooner or later. She put on her hat and secured the chin strap. Then she picked up her pack and insect net and started picking her way through the vegetation along the side of the mountain.

She had gone perhaps 20 feet when she heard it. There was almost no warning this time. The earth's thunder came a split second before she was violently thrown from her feet into the brush. There was no time to think, no time to get ready. There was no time to feel that awful foreboding that people well acquainted with earthquakes feel; that instant when the deep roar of the earth presages the shaking to come. Both seemed to hit almost together. She thought the entire mountain was falling. Lung-choking dust was heavy in the air. She got to her feet but it was difficult to remain standing. It was like water-skiing on land. The earth was making waves and she was nauseated. Her knees were weak and she stood in a half-crouch, holding on to the brush next to her. After an interminable time, it stopped. Everything but the wind.

"Oh my God," she cried. She must get back to the car, pick up Susan and Phil and get back home.

"I wonder if the road down the mountain is passable," she murmured to herself. "There are probably rock slides. I hope Susan and Phil are okay." Her knees were steadier now and she started up the hill toward the car.

Dr. Peter Chin had been busy all morning finalizing a paper he was going to read at the seismology meetings next week in San Francisco. One thing about working for the U.S.

Geological Survey, there was plenty of time to do research and write up the results. The problem was that earthquakes don't occur when and where you want them to and so finding a good research project was kind of chancy. You took what you got when you got it. He wished that the small earthquake yesterday on the Cucamonga fault had occurred several weeks earlier so that he could have done some measurements and reported on that. Instead, his report was on some pretty theoretical stuff based on data he had gathered here and there. Deep down inside he felt fairly sure that the paper was not very interesting or significant. But, anyway, he would give the report and decide later whether it was publishable. Perhaps he could refine the data in some way before submitting the paper to a publisher.

Peter usually made an effort to attend several scientific meetings each year, even though he could only produce perhaps one, or at most two, papers to read. But he enjoyed listening to what other people had to report. And he especially enjoyed the social contact with other seismologists, some of whom he knew from college days. Moreover, it was always nice to get away from the routine of his office. Once in a while his wife went with him, but only when she could get time off from her job. She was not going this time, but most of the Geological Survey people from here were going, and several seismologists from Caltech across the street. Everyone would probably fly to San Francisco together and it would be a fun trip.

Peter was starting to rehearse his talk for the third time when it happened. He heard the rumble, then his office began to rock. His desk chair, which was on wheels, gave him a wild ride around the room. He sat in it transfixed as if in a dream. The chair skidded from one side of his office to the other. Books were thrown from his bookcases. One whole top shelf of books came down on his head and shoulders. Fortunately, the cases had been secured to the wall throughout the building in preparation for just such an occurrence. Otherwise, he could have been severely injured. Finally, his senses came back to him and he decided he'd better get out into the hall where there was no moving furniture to hit him.

Above the roar of the earth, he could hear windows shattering throughout the building. There were crashes he couldn't identify, probably pictures falling or equipment overturning and falling off tables and stands. One woman was screaming from somewhere downstairs. The building was creaking and groaning, but it was a wood frame and had been built decades ago with strength in mind, and Peter felt safe enough.

After what he guessed might be 25 or 30 seconds, the motion stopped. Peter now had his wits about him and he put into action the routine that the staff had discussed a couple of times in the event of a bad earthquake. First he would check to see if anyone in the building was injured or trapped. Everyone else appeared to be doing the same thing. He could hear a woman's sobbing downstairs, but someone coming up the stairs as he was going down said she was okay, just frightened. After he was sure no one was in trouble, he headed back to his office to see what could be salvaged.

The electricity had gone off momentarily, but the backup generator for the Geological Survey buildings had kicked in, and the lights and instruments were back on again. He should get a report via an electronic paging radio link with Caltech at any minute. The report would indicate the epicenter and a magnitude that would be too low. The true magnitude for such a large earthquake would take longer. It was coming through now. The epicenter was a couple of miles northwest of Claremont.

He lifted the phone receiver, listened in vain for a dial tone, and replaced the receiver. He would not try to call his wife. He could probably not get through anyway, and they had agreed long ago that they would not try to phone each other if a large quake happened. She would not be expecting a call from him, and she would not be expecting him home until she saw him at the front door. He would have duties to perform.

Peter had picked up about half of his books when the

update report came in from Caltech. He already knew just about what the pager would say. The epicenter from the earlier report and the length of the quake told him it was probably on the Sierra Madre fault. No other fault in the vicinity was large enough for such a long duration. The pager indicated the magnitude was somewhere between 7.0 and 7.3. Exact magnitude would be available in another 15 or 20 minutes. Yesterday must have been a fore shock. It was a warning of today's big one, Peter thought, and we are still so ignorant of seismic events that we could not call it. Then another thought occurred to him. There would be no meeting at San Francisco next week. Or if there was, no one from Pasadena would be there.

 ELEVEN

Phil and Susan stared at each other unbelievingly. Could the chaparral be on fire? They had just come through a severe earthquake, now were they going to have to face a brush fire? In this wind it could be devastating, and it could travel faster than they could.

"The fire must be either north or east of here, Susan," reasoned Phil. "That's the direction the wind is blowing from, and we couldn't smell the smoke otherwise. But maybe it's miles away. In this wind the smoke could be coming from far away."

"What shall we do, Phil?" pleaded Susan. "What if it's not far away?"

Phil thought a moment. "We'd better get up to the road. Maybe we can outrun it on the road. We sure can't outrun it crawling through this brush." They started up the mountain. Susan's hat blew off again, but they let it go. There was no time to retrieve unnecessary items. Susan felt sick and desperate. It felt like a large, heavy stone had been placed in the pit of her stomach, and her legs were shaky. But when Phil asked her how she was doing and if she needed help, she said she was okay and didn't need assistance. Their clothes were soaked with sweat and their breathing was labored. The smell of smoke was much stronger now and they could see it blowing over them. Bits of gray and black ash were falling on them.

"Phil, can't we leave our packs? Why do we have to carry them?" gasped Susan.

"Right. Let's drop everything but our canteens. We have to have water."

They rested a minute, trying to control their breathing. Phil looked worried now. Obviously, the fire was close or there wouldn't be this much smoke or ash. He was uncertain whether they were doing the right thing by climbing the hill. It was much slower then going down. Perhaps the road would do them little good anyway. The fire might be traveling faster than they could run. He just didn't know, but he said nothing that might worry Susan.

They started up the hill again, Phil holding Susan's hand, trying to help her as much as possible. The smoke was getting dense. It was multicolored; a blending of yellow, white, light brown and black. It was streaming over them at a high rate of speed, blowing southwestward toward the valley. It was like a giant sheet gradually enveloping them, being held close to the contour of the mountain because of the wind. Breathing was becoming terribly difficult now. Susan had to stop again, completely winded. "Phil, I'm scared!" she sobbed. She thought she was going to be all right until now. But now her body was letting her down. She wasn't certain she could drag it much farther. She had a fantasy, an irrational desire to leave it—go on without it.

"We'll rest a minute, sweetheart. You'll feel better in a minute," gasped Phil. "We're going to make it, I'm sure."

Susan tried to believe what he said, but her head was full of doubts. The fire was getting too close. The smoke was getting too thick and they were going the wrong direction, almost directly into the smoke instead of away from it.

When she had caught her breath a little, she said, "Phil, aren't we going the wrong way? We're going right into the fire. Why are we doing this?"

"Honey, I'm trying to get up to the road where we can move fast. We can outrun it there. We can get out of its way. If we go downhill, there's nothing but brush down there."

"But it's terribly hard going up."

"I know, but I'll help you and we'll make it. We're probably halfway to the road already." They started upward again.

Janice stopped climbing. She thought she could smell smoke. She took a moment to look around; there *was* smoke in the air. "Oh, please God, not a fire!" she pleaded. "Not a fire on top of all this." Excessive adrenaline surged in her body and made her nauseated. This could be a death trap for me, she thought. It depends on where the fire is and how fast its traveling. "I hope to God that Susan and Phil climbed up to the road a little early," she murmured to herself. "Maybe it's just a small fire and they're not in the path."

She tried to concentrate on what she had read about chaparral fires so she could decide what to do. She knew there was no chance of outrunning it in this wind, not through thick chaparral. The brush was so dry it would just explode when fire touched it. She felt her only chance was to reach the car. In the car she might be able to get out of its way, or at least the car would give her enough protection to survive. But what about Susan and Phil? There was no time to waste. She would try for the car even though it was uphill and in the general direction the smoke was coming from. She tried to look for passages where the brush was a little less thick. She could travel slightly faster there. She was surprised that most of the fear had left her. It had nearly consumed her for a few terrible moments after she had seen the smoke. Now the adrenaline was doing what it was supposed to do, giving her additional strength and energy.

She was astonished by her own courage. It was as if she were not totally involved, as if she were viewing this from a distance and was not terribly concerned. She would either make it or she wouldn't. If she didn't, the kids would go to her parents. She had discussed this with Jennifer and Todd, and she knew her parents would be perfectly willing to take on the responsibility if anything happened to her. She had no worries there. Right now she would put all her energy into activity and try to escape. For some odd reason she thought about the rattlesnake and the coyote. Of course! They knew the earthquake was coming. That's why they were acting so strangely. Other people had reported strange behavior from animals just before earthquakes.

The smoke and ash-fall were getting much thicker. The fire was closer than she wanted it to be. If she could just get to the top of this particular rise and look over its ridge, she might be able to see enough to tell her exactly where the fire was. With one last gigantic effort, she staggered to the top of the ridge and looked over.

There it was! She could see the fire. She realized instantly that she could not get to the car. In fact, the fire was burning right about where the car was parked. Her hope crumbled. She was probably going to die.

Susan was so tired she could barely keep going. Her legs were like rubber. Her lungs were bursting. Phil was getting tired now too, but he wouldn't admit it to himself. He tried to help Susan as much as possible, but he had only so much energy, only so much strength. His leg muscles felt dead. He would have carried her, but he knew that he could not. He realized now that their situation was desperate. There was very little chance of their reaching the road before the fire did. He could see no spots where there might be a chance that they could "dig in" somehow and let the fire pass them by. No open clearing, no deep gully where the fire, in its wind blown haste, might jump over them. He looked at Susan. Her face was frozen. No emotion, no feeling. She had given up. She already knew what their fate was to be.

Phil would not give up. They were still alive and they would battle this thing until the very end. He didn't let himself think what it might be like to die in a fire. Somehow he had to get Susan to safety. It didn't matter about him. Fire was "spotting" everywhere now. Flaming bunches of leaves, branches and debris were being swept by the wind ahead of the main conflagration. Each flaming brand would eventually settle and start a new fire of its own. There were small fires all around them, and even though the smoke was thick, he could see that there was spotting behind them where they had just come from.

Susan had stopped and sat down. Phil screamed to her above the howl of the wind to get up and follow him. She must not stop now. She must follow his instructions. What the hell did she think she was doing? He would get her to safety if she would only get up. Just like a goddamned woman to quit! Suddenly, he was furious, a raging madman that could not accept defeat and death. He shrieked at Susan to get off her ass and get going! Did she want to get them both killed? Susan lifted her head a little and he could see her eyes, but there was no life in them. He wasn't even sure she recognized him, or even knew that he was there. It was as if she were already dead.

It was getting unbearably hot now. The roar of the wind-driven fire storm was mind-numbing. It was like being inside a jet engine when the airplane was taking off. He had to lean hard against the wind to keep standing. Phil could hardly see. His eyes were full of smoke and ashes. They burned terribly. He couldn't breath. He turned from looking at Susan to look at the raging fire above and in front of him. He stared transfixed. The inferno seemed to be leaping in all directions. Great tongues of flame 40 feet long were reaching out toward him, blown horizontally by the cyclone behind them. Dense clouds of preheated, flammable gas were exploding in front of the flaming brush. He was mesmerized by the cataclysm. He knew now that they could not escape. He knew that this would be the last and greatest spectacle that they would ever witness here on earth. He would finally have to accept what Susan had already accepted. This was to be their last few minutes alive together. Perhaps some part of their spirits or souls or essence would be carried to some other place or some other time, but their present state of existence was about to end.

He turned and worked his way back to Susan's side. She seemed all but lifeless now. He wrapped his arms around her shoulders and his bitter tears fell on her face. He turned his back to the flames. He did not want to see them any more.

Now everything was turning red, bright red! He closed his eyes. His body began to convulse in the heat and raging noise. Finally, they seemed to overpower him. He lurched over, partly covering Susan's body with his own, and experienced an intensely white light as his central nervous system over-heated.

Janice was caught! She could see only two possibilities of surviving. Either she had to find some passage through the fire and get over to where it had already burned, or she had to hole up somehow and let it burn over her. She tried to look for some kind of a break in the wall of fire that was rapidly approaching. There was nothing that she could see. It seemed to be a solid wall of flames and smoke. Probably no hope there. That left the other option, to somehow survive its passing over her. But how? She needed a cave or something to hide in. Something to insulate her from the heat that could sear her lungs and the smoke that could choke her. There would also be a lack of oxygen and too much carbon monoxide. Fat chance of finding a cave now that she needed one. She had noticed shallow overhangs in rocky outcroppings during her weeks of working in the mountains, but there was nothing like that in this particular place. However, there was what looked like an outcropping of large rocks perhaps two hundred yards away on the same ridge where she was standing. The ridge angled upward and to the right.

She began climbing toward the rocks. The brush was considerably thinner at the top of the ridge making the going easier. She wondered how much time she had before the fire would be here. Not long, she judged, from the way it was progressing. Yes, it seemed to be a rather large outcropping of rocks right at the very top of the ridge. Weathering had worn the soil away, and there was very little brush surrounding the rocks. Only a stunted plant here and there where there was a bit of dirt to grow in. But there was no real shelter. Only the rocky ridge open to the sky, like the exposed vertebrae of some giant, fossil animal. How could she protect herself from the flames if she took shelter here? Build a sort of cave from the rocks? No, it was obvious that she could not do that. The rocks were not loose, and there was no time anyway.

Suddenly, she thought of her pack. She still had her pack with her, hadn't even thought about dropping it somewhere to get rid of the weight. And inside the pack was the aluminum cover that she always carried. A cover to keep her warm in case she was obliged to spend the night somewhere in the mountains. Now she needed something to keep her cool enough to survive a raging fire. Maybe it would work. She remembered reading somewhere about forest fire fighters having to carry aluminum-cloth shelters with them. It was mandatory. Lives had been saved by using them. She didn't know what the shelters were like or how they were used exactly, but she thought the article said that the person would lay down and hold the shelter over his body. She might be able to do that with her cover.

The fire was getting close. Her eyes smarted terribly and she was coughing from smoke inhalation. She needed something to protect her mouth and nose from the smoke. Was there anything in her pack she could use? She could tear a strip from her shirt that she could tie around her head. But maybe she had something else just as good. She took two large pieces of gauze out of the first aid kit in her pack.

These would have to serve the purpose. She could tape

them tight to her face using bandage tape. She emptied her pack and unfolded the aluminum-cloth. She could wet her clothing with the water left in her canteen. But she might need the water to drink. Besides, the moisture could scald her skin in case her clothing got too hot.

Janice picked the most protected spot she could find in the rocks. It was a long, fairly narrow crevice lying parallel to the line of the fire. On the side from which the fire was coming, there was a nearly perpendicular wall of rock about three feet high. This, she hoped, would protect her somewhat from the force of the wind and flames. The rock wall on the other side sloped upward more gradually and was only about half as high. This spot was the best she could find. She glanced at the inferno rushing toward her. She had perhaps two minutes to get ready. She tried to ignore the increasing heat and noise. She cleared several clumps of dry grass from the crevice so there was nothing left but bare stone and dirt. She managed to find a single, large rock that was loose enough so it could be pried from its surroundings, and put it on top of one end of the aluminum cover. It would help to hold the cover down at the end where her feet would be. She knew there would be tornado-like winds as the fire passed over. Somehow, she must hold the cover down. Then she got under the cover and carefully folded the bottom end under her feet. She hoped her booted feet and the rock would be enough to hold the cover. Then she emptied her pack and placed it partway over her head for extra protection. The last thing she did was to fold the sides and top end of the aluminum cover under enough so that her arms and hands and head could hold it down. She had to hold her position, putting all her weight on the under-folded parts of the cover.

Now she waited, but not long. She wanted to close her eyes, but they would not cooperate. The noise crescendoed, the wind ripped at her shelter. She saw the intense red glow right through the shelter. There was one terrific blast of wind that she was certain would tear the cover away. The heat grew unbearable and she was afraid that she could not remain conscious. Then gradually, the raging storm lessened. She gasped for air. She was alive! She had made it, but she would remain motionless a while longer just in case. She waited for what seemed endless time. She was jubilant. She was actually alive and there was hope again. But now her entire body was shaking. Now that the worst seemed to be over, her courage was gone and she was losing control.

Janice cautiously lifted one corner of her cover and looked out. She could see nothing but the rock wall on one side of the crevice where she lay. She opened more of the shelter and got up on her hands and knees. The world had changed colors. The browns and greens of the chaparral had been replaced with blacks and grays and still-burning reds. The contents of her pack, that she had emptied on the rocks, were either burned or had been turned into rubbish. The collecting bottles were shattered from the heat. Her collecting net that she had carried all the way with her was nothing more than a metal rim. The wooden handle had burned and the nylon mesh had melted. Her canteen she had drawn to safety under the shelter. She took a drink of the hot water it contained. It helped to wash down some of the ashes and grit that clogged her mouth and throat. She looked around. The main wall of fire was moving away from her now, toward the valley. Some of the larger trunks and branches of the burned chaparral were still standing, either blackened and smoking, or still birthing flames that whipped like ghostly, scarlet colored flags in the wind. Everything else was ashes. She would not be able to move away from the rocks until things cooled off a little. It might take a while. Then she would begin looking for her two students.

TWELVE

FIRESCOPE was a mass of confusion. Joe Agramonte was desperately trying to turn that confusion into something that made a little more sense. Messages were coming in from a great many locations; reports of structural fires that had started as a result of the earthquake, and pleas for assistance when local fire fighting units were unable to handle their problems. Most areas reported no electricity. Watermains had apparently been broken by the quake since many areas reported no water. Water was especially scarce along the foothills of the San Gabriel Mountains where the ground had been ruptured near the fault. Many fires had been started by broken gas lines, overturned water heaters, downed power lines, every possible situation where something combustible came in contact with a spark or flame. Without water, there wasn't much the fire control people could do.

But what frightened Joe was the wind. Most areas were reporting northeast winds of anywhere from 35 to 70 miles per hour. The worst had happened! A large earthquake had occurred at a time when the Santa Anas were blowing. Some said it would never happen. What were the odds of a severe earthquake coming along just when the Santa Ana winds happened to be kicking up? It was the nightmare that every disaster agency in Southern California dreaded. What could be done under conditions like these? Even in those areas that still had water pressure, fire control was problematic. The wind, by and large, dictated what the fires would do. Other environmental factors played along with the wind. Temperatures were high throughout the region. Los Angeles was reporting 101 degrees, Ontario was 105 degrees and it wasn't even noon yet. Relative humidities were down to almost nothing, two to five percent in many places. Hot and dry enough to take the moisture out of almost anything combustible. The leaves of normally fire resistant plants would wilt under such conditions.

Besides the structural fires, there were several chaparral fires reported. The largest was in the San Gabriel Mountains southwest of Baldy Village and northeast of Claremont. This one had apparently started before the earthquake. Someone down in the valley near the base of Mount Baldy road had called in a sighting of smoke to the Lower San Antonio Forest Service Station just a minute or two before the earthquake. "Arsonist," said Joe to himself. "Some son of a bitch started that fire. I'll bet my life on it. I hope whoever it was burns in hell."

Most of the reports were coming in by radio since the telephones weren't working. People were in and out of Joe's building. He could hear the front door opening and slamming shut every few moments. Vehicles were being started out in front and driven off. Some had their sirens on before they hit the front gate.

Another report of a brush fire was just coming in. This one

was in the foothills near Glendora. The Dalton Hotshot firecrew, stationed nearby, was on it already. Good luck to you guys, Joe thought. I don't know what you can do to stop it.

Many of the fire suppression crews had been cut in strength. Budget problems were the reason. Both federal and state funding were affected. The U. S. Forest Service's eight expert fire fighting crews—known as Hotshots—in Southern California had been cut to half their normal strength. The California Department of Forestry and the county fire crews had been cut even more drastically. Some fire stations had been closed. They were having to rely on moving smaller crews longer distances to fires rather than having a crew near at hand. "It makes you feel very vulnerable," was the statement from one of the fire control supervisors. "It's just about guaranteed that any fire that starts in Santa Ana winds will be blown toward houses. The only way you have a fighting chance of containing these fires is to get there fast. The way things are now we won't be getting there as fast. We've got a program here with about two-thirds of the necessary dollars to fund it. We're several million dollars short. If fewer people show up at a fire, and if it takes longer to get there, houses will burn."

The fire that Joe was most concerned about was the one northeast of Claremont. It must have been started by an arsonist somewhere near the Mount Baldy road and was burning directly toward the city of Claremont, which at its north end, was jammed right up against the foothills. Whoever the nut was that started this one, thought Joe, he knew what he was doing. Joe lived in Riverside, but he and his wife had friends who lived in the older part of Claremont, not far from the Claremont Colleges. Every time they went to visit their friends, Joe shook his head. What a perfect firetrap the place was. Many of the buildings were old, most of them made of wooden siding, some with wooden shakes or shingles on the roofs. Eucalyptus trees had been planted throughout the area. Some of the trees were gigantic. Eucalyptus trees were oily, and even when alive, were extremely combustible. Pine trees and other conifers were common also, and they were full of resin. Both kinds of trees would burn like massive torches, throwing flames hundreds of feet into the air if they ever got started. Shrubbery was everywhere around these old buildings, much of it burnable.

The Claremont Colleges were somewhat better off since many of the buildings were new and fire resistant. However, there were some old buildings on the campuses too, and many eucalyptus and coniferous trees. Just north of the colleges was the Rancho Santa Ana Botanic Garden. If fire got in there on a windy day, it would roar right through the place since the vegetation was thick. Joe was very concerned. A large wind-driven fire was roaring directly toward this vulnerable spot. It would hit there and continue on to the west where the communities of La Verne and San Dimas were located.

The last reports from all three locations indicated they had no water pressure. The reports also indicated extensive earthquake damage. What could be done?

About all he could do was to direct as many fire fighting units to this fire as possible. But there would be problems. There were many other fires out of control. There would be few units available, and most units would not want to leave their own areas anyway, with the danger of new fires starting at any time. Air units were out of the question. Neither air tankers nor helicopters could fly in this wind. He thought about the 1991 Oakland fire. The only thing that stopped that one was the fact that the wind died and marine air began flowing into the area. And *they* had water!

Reports of two new brush fires were just coming in over the radio, both of them out of control. The Glendora fire was also running out of control. Joe could sense a real disaster here. He would have to request fire fighting units from other parts of California. He would also put in a request to the National Coordination Center at Boise for help from other states. Whether they could get here in time was the problem. But he would call them anyway. What other option did he have?

• • •

Janice felt she could wait no longer. A great deal of heat was still radiating from the burned area around her. She was mostly worried about her feet since the ashes were still pretty hot and she would have to wade through them. But she would give it a try. If her boots got too hot she would just have to find a spot to stop and wait a little longer. She would stay on the ridges as much as possible. The ashes would be more shallow there since the brush had not been as tall or as thick in those places. Also the wind was blowing most of the ashes away from the exposed ridges.

There was not much reason to take her backpack since most everything that had been in it was burned or beyond repair. She tried to think, however, whether she might have a use for the pack itself later on. She could carry things in it. But what would there be to carry? She didn't know. She finally decided to take it, and she folded the aluminum cover and put it inside. She wasn't sure she wanted to part with something that had saved her life. Her Swiss army knife had survived the fire, so she stuck it in her pocket. Janice knew that her car had been destroyed, but she wanted to see it anyway. Besides, it would be just as quick to get to the road going that way as any other. She would go to the road, inspect the car, then head up the road in the direction of where Susan and Phil should be.

What if she didn't find them? She didn't even want to think about that. They just *had* to be safe. She couldn't bring herself to think about what she would do if they were not. Her mind went numb at that point.

She started up the ridge. She could feel the heat of the hot ground and ashes almost immediately through her boots and she wondered whether she would have to wait a while longer. But that was the last thing she wanted to do, so she kept going. The heat was intense. The hot wind buffeted her body. It was blowing clouds of ashes and debris directly at her. She tried to shield her eyes as much as possible with her hands and arms. Her gauze mask was still in place over her mouth and nose. She was desperately thirsty but didn't have very much water left in her canteen and didn't know when or where she could get more. After a few minutes it appeared that her feet would not be badly burned. A few blisters probably, nothing more. She trudged doggedly up the slope with the sun bearing down from above, the heat radiating upward from the scorched earth below, and the dreadful hot wind coming from in front. She felt light-headed but fought off the feeling. She would get to the road somehow and then it would be a little easier going. She began to hallucinate. She thought she could hear Phil and Susan calling to her. She stopped to listen. Nothing! Only the howl of the wind. She didn't remember the rest of the climb. All of a sudden, there was her car—what remained of it. The windows had been shattered by the heat. The inside was burned out. One tire was still burning. The paint had burned off. She hardly recognized it.

Janice lifted the gauze mask from her mouth just enough to take two small swallows of water and turned toward where Phil and Susan should be. Perhaps it had not even burned where they were. Perhaps they were looking for her, and in a minute she would see them walking down the road toward her. She tried to readjust the gauze mask without removing any of the tape because she knew the tape would not stick again and she did not have any more. To shield her eyes better she took her hat off and held it down low on her forehead. That way, not so much debris would blow directly into her face. Now she could walk fairly fast even though she was going almost directly into the teeth of the wind. It took her perhaps 20 minutes to walk to where the large pine tree had been. Its skeleton was still there, a smoking, blackened sentinel that told her Phil and Susan had not been beyond the range of the fire.

No sign of them. What now? Could they have come up to the road and walked in the other direction? Or perhaps they found a way to dodge the fire down where they were working. They had been quite a ways down the mountain. Even though it burned up here, maybe it hadn't burned down there. Or maybe they found shelter and were still there. She tried to calm herself enough to make a rational decision about what to do.

Try to walk out and find help to look for them? Or go down herself and try to locate them? If she did that, would her water last?

Janice realized suddenly that she could not just walk away without knowing what happened to the two students. She would have to at least try to find them. After all, who would be available to help look for them? Everyone would have his own problems after an earthquake and fire. She thought she knew approximately what their route would be in coming back up to the road. Everything looked different since the fire, but she thought she could find her way. She left her pack on the road with a rock on top of it so it wouldn't blow away. Then she started down. She called their names, but the wind just seemed to engulf her calls and absorb them. She listened carefully. There was no answer. She continued downward, calling as she went. The ashes were cooler now. The heat was not quite so unendurable.

She was nearly halfway down now and still nothing. Then a curious looking mound caught the corner of her eye, off to the left perhaps twenty yards away. Or was it two mounds, one almost on top of the other. She wanted a closer look. She was perhaps ten yards from the curiosity when she stopped dead still. The hair on the back of her neck stood up. She knew instinctively that she had found what she desperately wanted *not* to find. Then she saw the remains of a blackened arm and hand sticking out from the mound. She stood there in shock. A low moan began way deep in her throat. It grew in volume. An anguished cry developed from the moan. A series of animal-like screams followed. The wind carried them down the mountain. Then she dropped to her knees in the still hot ashes and sobbed uncontrollably. They had died in the fire, and she alone was responsible for their deaths.

THIRTEEN

It was 12:30 P.M. Four fire crews were working the brush fire roaring toward Claremont. But there was almost nothing they could do. It was too dangerous to get in front of the fire since the wind was driving it so rapidly. They had to work from the flank, trying to keep it from moving southward into the housing areas. Even so it was very dangerous and frustrating work. The conflagration was over a mile wide at its front. One end of the front was racing down the west side of San Antonio Wash. The other end had burned over Potato Mountain to Chicken Canyon and was heading into Palmer Canyon. Palmer Canyon had been evacuated; the northern sections of Claremont were in the process of being evacuated.

It wasn't a single fire anymore. Spot fires had developed to the south and west of the main front. Flaming firebrands were being hurled more than half a mile by the wind. If they happened to land on something burnable, a new fire started. Most of the activity of the firefighters was concentrated on intercepting these spot fires and trying to put them out before they got a foothold. The fire crews were constantly being pushed southward and were on the outskirts of Claremont now. As the fire got closer, more and more burning debris would be blown, leapfrog fashion, into the city and land on wooden roofs, wooden decks, piles of scrap lumber, fireplace wood, wooden fences, pine needles caught in roof gutters, combustible shrubs and trees, dry grassy areas, door mats, anything that would burn. For every new fire contained, ten others would escape containment. The only water available was from tanker trucks and swimming pools. The situation was critical. Within one-half hour, Claremont would be burning. Unless a massive amount of help arrived very quickly, it all seemed hopeless.

Fortunately, some of the newer housing developments were fairly well protected. Most of these buildings had noncombustible roofs and walls. Shrubbery tended to be scarce around them. But there were many older subdivisions at the edge of the city that were unprotected. And once the flames got into the still older, central part of Claremont, where almost everything was burnable, a firestorm would result. It was a powder keg waiting to blow up.

Joe Agramonte at FIRESCOPE was receiving reports that the brush fire near Glendora, west of Claremont, was now spotting into the city. And west of Glendora there were a couple of fires, apparently started by downed electrical wires, that were burning toward Pasadena and Altadena. Both cities had build homes and businesses right next to brushy and wooded areas. The fires were wildland fires now, but houses would become the fuel for them very shortly. There were calls for assistance from units fighting virtually every fire that was burning nearest the earthquake area. Most of their water delivery systems had been disrupted by the shaking.

• • •

Janice was working her way down the main road from the mountain. Her watch said 5:55 P.M. It was beastly hot and the wind was still gusting as hard as ever. She had seen no one on the road. It was impassable for automobiles because of numerous landslides. She had come upon several vehicles that had apparently been on the road when the earthquake hit. They were trapped between slides so they could go neither up nor down the mountain. They were locked and abandoned. The people that had occupied them were on foot just as she was. She found a little water in the creek bed at the bottom of the canyon below the road. She didn't know if it would make her sick if she drank it, but her thirst was so demanding that she didn't care. It's probably loaded with *Giardia* or some other parasites, she thought to herself. But it tasted like heaven and she drank deeply.

As she looked over the valley there seemed to be smoke everywhere, as if everything was burning. It would be dark by the time she got home if she had to walk all the way. She wondered if she still had a home. Had the earthquake destroyed it? There must be at least some damage, she thought. Maybe it has burned to the ground in the fires. But mostly she didn't care about the house as long as the kids were safe. Her anxiety about her children, the shock of nearly being killed in the fire and her extreme fatigue magnified her remorse about the deaths of Susan and Phil. Her nervous system could handle just so much tragedy all at once.

Twenty minutes later she was trudging down the road when she saw someone coming up the road toward her. She assumed it was someone who lived in Baldy Village, trying to get home. As the figure grew larger, she suddenly sensed something familiar about it. She stopped and stared. The figure started running toward her. Oh God! It was Tony!

Tony had come to find her. She was running now too. And crying. She tried desperately not to, but she was bawling like a baby. Tony's face was mixture of joy and relief. He wrapped his arms around her and held her as if he could never let go. She let her body go totally limp in his embrace so that he was supporting all her weight.

"Oh darling, I was so afraid for you," he was saying. "I was so horribly afraid." She could say nothing. He held her and soothed her.

"It's all right, Janice. Everyone is okay. Todd and Jenny are just fine. We were so worried about you that I just had to come and try to find you." He kissed her face that was streaked with smoke, dirt and tears.

They clung to each other for perhaps a full minute, saying nothing, just grateful to have each other. When Janice finally calmed down enough to talk she said, "Tony, thank you for coming. Are my children alright? You've seen them?"

"Sure I've seen them. And they're great. They wanted awfully to come with me, but I thought it would be better if they didn't. I had real trouble getting Todd convinced he should stay and take care of his sister. But he finally agreed, and they're both over at Mrs. Lavins. She and Jennifer were pretty upset by the quake, so they're consoling each other. Todd is more upset about his missing mother, so we've got to get you home as soon as possible so both of your kids can see you." Tony held Janice away from him and scrutinized her.

"By the way, you're kind of a mess," he said with the barest trace of a grin. "We'll have to find some soap and water and some clean clothes for you. Can you walk to the car, do you think? You look like you've been through hell."

"I have, Tony, I have," she croaked. "Susan and Phil are dead. I killed them." She said it so quietly that he wasn't sure he had heard correctly over the noise of the wind. He stared at her stunned.

"What?" he said.

She couldn't say all of it again, so she just said, "I killed them."

He realized instantly that she was treading the bare edge of sanity. Apparently she knew, or at least thought she knew that her assistants were dead, and she was blaming herself. He understood very little about psychology, but his common sense told him he had to treat this problem very carefully or

Janice might go off the deep end. He decided he had better try to lead her from the subject, at least for right now. Funny, he was just going to ask her about Susan and Phil. He was glad that he hadn't. Something terrible must have happened up there on the mountain; or, at least Janice thought something terrible had happened. He had to get more information from her about the students in case they needed help, but he would wait at least a few minutes until she was more like herself. He led her over into the shade of the high bank beside the road. They sat down there. He kept talking softly just to ease her mind and he wanted her to rest a few minutes. She leaned against him and closed her eyes. He held her gently. After a few minutes she opened her eyes. She looked a little better.

"Janice," he said, "I must ask you something."

"I know," she answered. "It's about my students."

He nodded. "I have to know if they need my help. I can't leave here until I know. You told me a few minutes ago that they are beyond my help. Are you sure that is true? Or did they just disappear and you're not sure what happened to them?"

She began to cry again. "I'm so sorry, my darling," he said. "I don't want to put you through this."

After a moment she gathered herself together enough to make the statement she knew he had to hear. She choked it out. "I found their bodies; they are dead." He looked deeply into her eyes and knew that what she said was true. Then uncontrollably sobs shook her entire body. He held her a long time until she stopped shaking.

"Now we'll go home," he said. He kissed her and helped her to her feet. They started walking down the road, hand in hand.

Tony had driven his car as far as he could in search of Janice. He had been stopped by the police at the foot of Mount Baldy road. The officer said the road was closed. No one could go into the area. So he had turned around, driven back the way he had come until he was out of sight of the police, found a place to park his car and started walking. He evaded the police blockade by walking up the bottom of the canyon, out of sight. As soon as he felt it was safe, he climbed back up to the road. He had gone only three or four miles before he spotted Janice. Now, they had to go back to the car.

They talked a little on the way back. She wanted to know about her children and the house. He tried to keep as positive as possible about everything. He told Janice that after the quake, he had thought about Jennifer and Todd since he knew their mother was in the mountains. So he drove to their house. Todd was there. He was fine. Together they went to Jennifer's school and picked her up. The school authorities were holding all the kids until someone came for them. Jennifer had been terribly upset by the earthquake, but Tony toned down the version he gave to Janice. He just said she was fine—a little scared. Then they had gone back to Janice's house. The house was in pretty good shape, a few windows broken, some cracks in the inside walls, some stucco fallen from the outside walls. Nothing had caved in. Of course, the furniture had been rearranged, pictures had fallen, cupboards had emptied, that sort of thing. Together they had straightened up some of the mess.

As the day wore on, they had become increasingly worried about Janice. Jennifer was also worried about her sitter, Mrs. Lavin. Since the telephone system was down, they had gone over to Mrs. Lavin's house. She was all right but a little scared. They pitched in and helped her clean up some of the damage to her home. Todd and Jennifer had wanted to go looking for their mother, but finally Tony had persuaded Jennifer that she should stay with Mrs. Lavin. She wouldn't stay without Todd, so Tony had to persuade Todd to stay also. He finally convinced Todd that a "man" needed to be around—just in case. He promised both children that he would not return without their mother.

Then Janice asked Tony about his own house. He told her the truth, that he didn't know about it. He had left home just as the evacuation orders were being given. A police car had driven by his house with its loudspeaker issuing orders for everyone to leave because a fire was burning in their direction. He had grabbed his important papers, all the money he had in the house, some extra clothes, a few personal items, and he had left. The house had suffered extensive physical damage, being so close to the epicenter of the earthquake. Not just broken windows and cracks in the walls. Part of the back of the house had buckled and caved in. Fortunately, he had been in the front of the house ready to leave for the university when the earthquake struck. He didn't tell Janice, but he had very little hope that the house had been spared from burning. From what he had been able to ascertain from reports over his car's radio, the house must have been directly in the path of the fire. The radio said that it had burned right through the heart of Claremont. They had been unable to stop it. He couldn't understand his own feelings, but he really wasn't very interested in whether the house was still there. He fully expected to see a big bare spot where the building had been, and he didn't seem to care.

They finally reached Tony's car. The barricade was still at the foot of the road, but the police were gone. Tony would try to find a safer way to get back to Janice's house than the way he had come. He said there were some insane drivers out there. None of the stoplights were working because there was no electricity. The pavement was badly broken in most of the roads; some were impassable. A few minutes later they were going through the northern extension of Claremont. Many of the houses in this area were new and palatial.

"Rich people must live here," Janice said to Tony.

Most of the buildings had survived the fire in fairly good shape. There had been nothing much to burn. Very little wood in their surface structure, no large trees or shrubbery. The fire had skipped right over most of them. However, they could see evidence of extensive earthquake damage since the houses had been built very near the fault. Some of them were nothing but ruins. They wondered where all the people were. They saw only two or three. It was like a ghost town.

As the pair made their way further into the city, they began to see the kind of ruin and destruction they had not thought possible. There was only smoldering rubble where homes had been. Massive eucalyptus trees were reduced to blackened skeletons, some of them still burning. These giants must have been like huge torches as the fire came through, carrying flame from one tree to the next, from one house to the next.

Here and there part of a chimney still stood, the only monument left to mark a home, shaken first, then burned to the ground. But in most places where homes had been, there was nothing standing. They saw how forces of destruction act in curious ways. There were a few houses that had survived the fire, totally unscathed. They were scattered, seemingly no pattern to them. Some may have been more fire resistant with tile roofs and stucco walls, but one or two had wood shingles and all the things that should make them vulnerable. These must have been spared for other, unimaginable reasons. The gods work in mysterious ways, Janice thought. They took Susan and Phil, but spared me. They ravished most of this community, yet they left a few scattered homes untouched. Why? Are some things destined to survive? She could not believe it. It's just the draw of the cards, she thought. And sometimes it's luckier to lose. Sometimes to survive and to endure is to be caught in hell.

They began to see people now. Perhaps some had stayed throughout the fire storm, hoping to save their homes and possessions. Most had probably returned after the fire front had passed. They drove by two mummylike objects in the street. They looked like they were bodies that had been wrapped in blankets. Perhaps they were something else. Janice had tried to put Susan and Phil out of her mind temporarily; but now, after seeing these objects, the horror of finding the two dead students came back to haunt her. She wondered why there were no authorities in evidence. She had to report her students' deaths.

"Don't the police always patrol areas like these after a disaster?" she mumbled to Tony.

"Perhaps there are not enough of them; they're spread too

thin," answered Tony. "They will be back later. This thing has overwhelmed them."

A few minutes later Janice was nearly home. Fire had not affected this area. The main conflagration had not come this far south. The wind had blown it in a westerly direction before it got here. It was still burning to the west; she could see the great carpet of smoke in that direction. Tony pulled up in front of Mrs. Lavin's house. As exhausted as she was, Janice ran up to the front door. Mrs. Lavin was there to open it. Suddenly Jennifer, then Todd appeared from the back of the house. "Mama!" Jennifer screamed. Janice's body swayed for a moment. She tried desperately to stay upright by holding onto the door frame. She thought, I can't let go yet. Not yet. The next instant she was waking up on the floor. Her children were right there beside her. And so was Tony.

FOURTEEN

Janice was lying awake in the half-light of dawn. It was the fourth day after the earthquake and fire. This was the first decent sleep she had had. She had slept six hours, straight through with no interruptions, no nightmares, no dreams. The nights before had brought her only fitfull sleep. During the night of her tragic experience on the mountain, there had been no sleep at all. She and Tony had sat up all night talking, and she, crying some. Jennifer had also been out in the same room with them since the child was too frightened to be alone in her bedroom. Todd seemed to take earthquakes in stride, no problems with him.

Without Tony, Janice thought she would have gone mad. They talked about so many things that first, never-ending night. The most painful thing had been the deaths of Susan and

Phil. Janice blamed herself for what had happened, but Tony made her see that she wasn't totally responsible. He reminded her of their conversation the night before the tragedy, the night all four of them had had dinner together. She had asked the two assistants whether they wanted to go up the next day and finish working the area where they had been. She didn't demand that they do it. She had asked them and both had decided that they wanted to go. It made her feel a little better even though she still felt largely responsible.

The day after the earthquake, Tony had returned to the site of his own home. He appeared at first to be reluctant to even see what had happened to it. Janice had to insist that he go. It was as if he had already decided the house was lost and he might as well make the best of it. Janice had wanted to go with him, but he wanted her to rest. She decided not to argue about it. When he got back he told her that there was no house. It had burned to the ground just as he had expected. All he found were shards of glass, lumps of melted and twisted metal, masses of blackened rubble. It was odd how calm and resigned he appeared to be about his loss. Janice was much more upset than he was. She thought how strangely people react to catastrophes. Everyone a little different. Tony had suffered what should have been a great loss, and yet he put it completely aside as if it didn't really matter. Of course, Janice had insisted that he stay in her house with her and the children. He asked her if she was sure there was room. She put her hand on his and said, "Tony, I won't let you go anywhere else. We have plenty of room. We want you here." He had lost nearly everything. Luckily, he had had time to gather together some clothes and personal items before he had evacuated.

They were literally camping now, even though they were living in the house. There was no electricity, no water, no gas. Telephones were not working. Janice had not been able to contact her parents in Santa Rosa, nor had Tony been able to get through to his in Ohio. Luckily, Janice had been wise enough to make some preparations for just such an emergency. She had stored over 50 gallons of water and a large stock of canned foods. She also had all of her camping equipment, including two white-gas lanterns and a cooking stove. They were eating the last of the food that had been in the refrigerator. Some had spoiled already. The hardest part was trying to get along on so little water. They were trying to limit themselves to a gallon a day per person, and they were actually using even less than that. Jenny was delighted that she didn't have to take daily showers. Todd, on the other hand, was miserable without his. He said he just felt dirty all the time. So did Janice and Tony, but they tried to ignore it.

There had been two rather substantial aftershocks of the large quake. Of course, each aftershock had set Jennifer off again. It seemed that just as they had her calmed down somewhat, another tremor would terrify her all over again. She refused to sleep alone, so she was sleeping with her mother, and Tony had taken her bed. The Santa Ana winds had subsided and the weather had cooled down, making it possible to control the fires. The loss of life had been devastating. Workers were still finding bodies, and the authorities had made no estimates yet of the total death and injury counts. Property loses were unbelievable. The fires had been much more destructive than the earthquake. Thousands of homes and other buildings had been burned. No one knew how many people were homeless. As Tony had said to Janice when they were talking about it one afternoon, "When you pack several million people into an area this small, sooner or later you're going to have a major disaster."

Tony had been able to contact the Sheriff's Department about the bodies of Phil and Susan. The man he had talked to was reluctant to get involved in recovering the bodies. He said they were totally swamped and simply could not handle anything else. Tony finally got angry and told the man that he knew they were overloaded, but whose responsibility was it? The man agreed eventually to do it, but Janice would have to go along, of course, to show them where to look. Tony agreed to this plan. They had completed the sad project yesterday. A helicopter had been furnished. Tony had gone along with

Janice and two men from the Sheriff's Department. The bodies were brought back and that made Janice feel a little better.

The Sheriff's Department had also agreed to notify the parents of the students concerning their deaths. Janice had wanted to do this herself, but she could not get through to them on the phone. Janice realized that eventually she would have to go to the parents and tell them exactly what had happened. She owed them that much even though it would mean implicating herself in their deaths. But it might help to relieve her feelings of guilt.

All four of them listened regularly to news reports over Tony's car radio. It would be several more days in some areas, perhaps weeks in many others, before services could be restored. It was going to take much longer than anyone had predicted, according to the radio. The estimates had all been too optimistic. There were too many people and too much area involved. Instructions over the radio said that everyone should refrain from driving except in emergencies, and stay home if possible. There were emergency centers set up for the homeless, but not nearly enough. Many people apparently had not bothered to prepare for a disaster. They had stored no food or water. They had no way to cook or heat food. They were nearly helpless.

Looting had begun in earnest the second night after the earthquake. Oddly enough, there was very little activity the first day and night, or the second day. It was as if everyone was too stunned at first by it all. The police were beginning to hope there would be no looting or shooting; but, of course, they were wrong. During the second night, after the looting intensified, a curfew was called by many cities in the basin. No one was to be on the streets unless he or she had a very good reason to be. This didn't stop the gangs from being out there, of course, and since the gangs were active, many others thought they should be too. Since the authorities were spread too thin to protect property, property owners were protecting their own. Some looters had already been shot or shot at, as had some property owners. It was armed warfare in many areas. Police, the National Guard and the Armed Forces had been called in from all over in an attempt to get things in hand.

Masses of people had left the Los Angeles basin; they began leaving immediately after the earthquake. Only two freeways were open, and they were gridlocked for hours on end. Some of these people had said they were not coming back. Janice had talked for a few minutes to the Mexican lady who lived next door. She told Janice that she knew of several families in the neighborhood who said they were heading back to Mexico and would not return. But Janice felt that most of them would come straggling back sooner or later.

Schools were closed until utilities could be restored, and safety checks made of the buildings. The opening of fall term at the university, originally scheduled to begin in just a few days, had been postponed for another few weeks. Janice and Tony had not yet been to the university to investigate the damage to their offices and laboratories. They were anxious to go, but the orders "do not drive" coming over the radio, deterred them. Besides, it was dangerous to drive. Stoplights were not yet functioning. And there were more than the average number of maniacs out there on those roads that were travelable. It was best just to stay home, at least until stoplights were working again.

Janice yawned and decided to get up and start doing something. It would keep her from thinking about Susan and Phil. She still could not think of them without crying. Tony was probably tired of her behavior, but so far he had been more than understanding. She wouldn't have been able to function without him. She was almost glad his house had been destroyed so that he was here with her. She knew now that she loved him deeply. She was also pretty sure that he was in love with her, judging from his behavior and actions. He had not told her in so many words that he loved her, but the things he did and how he did them spoke for him. After all, this was no time for romance, and he was intelligent enough to realize as much. She felt guilty just thinking about her love for him when she probably should be grieving more over Susan and Phil.

She glanced over at Jennifer asleep under the sheet. Good time to get up and get into the bathroom before anyone else was up. The bathroom now consisted functionally of a portable camping toilet and a gallon bottle of water that was to be used sparingly. The contents of the portable toilet were emptied when necessary into a deep hole that Todd had dug in the back yard. Janice wondered how people in apartments were dealing with sewage disposal. Sometimes it was really convenient to have a private backyard. She also wondered how long it would be before she could wash clothes. Tony was running out of anything clean to wear. They might have to spare him enough water so that he could rinse out at least his underclothes and his shirts and socks. Everyone else had enough spare clothing to go quite a bit longer. They all might just end up by having to wear their clothes dirty, and sleep in sheets that had not been changed. Janice was certain that her ancestors had not worried too much about this problem.

She got out of bed, went into the bathroom, used the portable toilet, washed her hands in as little water as possible, got dressed and went out into the kitchen. Today, breakfast would be partly from cans. She still had a little fresh fruit left that had not spoiled, but barely enough for breakfast. She would wait until Tony was up and see what he wanted to eat. The kids would probably sleep late. Right now, she would have a cup of coffee. She and Tony were limiting themselves to two cups a day in order to save water. She had both of hers in the morning so she could get going, she said; he had one in the morning for breakfast and one after lunch. She lit the camp stove and put the water on to heat. Just then Tony appeared in the kitchen doorway.

"Good morning, Janice. Get a little sleep?" he asked in a sympathetic voice, as if he expected her to say she had had another miserable night.

"Morning, Tony. Yes, I finally got some sleep. I feel much better." He came over to her.

"I've been pretty worried about you," he said softly.

"Fortunately, time takes care of most anything if you can just hold on." He took her hand. "Incidentally, I want to thank you for sharing your water, food and home. I shouldn't be taking advantage of you like this."

She took his hand in both of hers. "Tony, you don't need to thank me. I am the one who should be thanking you—for my sanity. Without you I think I would be completely mad by now. You've helped me so much. Anything and everything here in this house is yours."

He grinned. "Can I have your two kids?" he asked.

"No," she answered smiling. "But you don't want them anyway."

"I just knew you didn't mean it," he laughed. She was still clutching his hand. His grin faded. He bent over and lightly kissed her lips. Her hands went to his face, holding it. The two looked into each other's eyes for an extended moment—longing—but it could not be now.

"Want some coffee?" she asked finally.

"Sure do," he answered.

FIFTEEN

There wasn't much to do but wait. Janice was working on some lecture notes that needed to be revised. Tony's lecture notes were all at the university where, supposedly, they had survived. Luckily he hadn't had any at home where they would have been burned. A couple of his text books had been at home, but he could replace them easily. To pass the time, he had begun reading one of Janice's entomology books and also one of her novels. They spent much of their time on the back patio, reading and talking. Todd was also reading a book of Janice's. Todd loved to read; he always had, ever since he had first learned the words. Jennifer, on the other hand, was not much of a reader. She would rather watch television or play some of her taped music. Without electricity, she could not have either of these distractions and without them, time lay heavily on her hands. Several times a day she would ask her mother what she could do.

Janice suggested that she practice her flute. There was no doubt that Jennifer was musically inclined, so her mother had started her on the instrument when she was eight. Janice had played flute in grade school and all through high school. Since the music program at Jennifer's school was in shambles, Janice had taught her daughter the basics of flute playing herself. There was something called "band practice" at Jenny's school once a week, but it wasn't much help to the kids who were learning to play musical instruments. A few of the children, whose parents could afford it, were taking private lessons. Jennifer was doing very well, but of course, practice was sometimes a problem. At least, though, she seemed to have some talent for the instrument.

Todd had also started to learn a musical instrument some years back. His choice had been the alto saxophone. He had tried hard, but it became obvious that he just didn't have the interest or the right genes. He would never be rich or famous because of his saxophone virtuosity. It was almost with relief that Janice had returned the rented saxophone to the music store. The awful squawks and screeches that Todd could produce from the single reed instrument were almost unbelievable. The man at the music store had suggested that perhaps another instrument would be more appropriate. Perhaps a French horn or a trumpet or trombone. She thanked the man for his help, but declined all of his offers. Todd would probably be better off finding some pastime other than that of playing music.

Tony had volunteered to help out in the water and food distribution service center, which had been established at Jennifer's school, about three blocks away. He reported for work about 2:00 P.M. every day, and stayed until the work was done, perhaps 8:00 or 9:00 P.M. At least it was something to do, and he felt like he was helping out. He looked forward to doing something besides just reading. Tony felt that Janice was stable enough now to be on her own, and besides, the kids would be with her and could come and get him if he was needed. He thought it might be a good idea if Janice got involved in something—just to get her mind off of things—but she didn't think she was ready to deal with people just yet. Anyway, she had plenty to do revising her lectures and doing some reading for one of the courses she would be teaching this next term. Besides, she still felt absolutely exhausted, as if she might never again have the energy that she was used to having. And she was still so emotional that any little thing could start tears flowing. She needed to get a better grip on herself before taking on additional responsibilities. She hoped she would be better when school started.

They had cleaned and patched up the house pretty well the first days following the quake. Dishes and glasses had fallen from the kitchen cupboard onto the tile around the sink. There had been broken glass and china all over the kitchen. Cleaning this up was the first thing they had done. Several pictures had fallen off the walls; the glass had broken in three of them. Two table lamps had broken when they fell. A large mirror had fallen, but there was a rug to cushion its landing and it had not broken. Several windows were cracked or broken. The cracked ones were left as they were. All the pieces of glass were removed from the frames of those that had broken. Janice had a large piece of transparent, heavy plastic that was cut into window-size pieces. These were tacked over the window frames. It might be weeks before things like window panes could be purchased. The house was livable but inconvenient without utilities.

Meals came largely out of cans. Dinner tonight would consist of canned tuna, canned green beans, fried potatoes and canned peaches. It was getting on toward that time. Janice put away her lecture notes and closed the book she had been reading. She wasn't sure she agreed with some of the things the author said, but anyway his views would make interesting discussion material in class. The two children had been very quiet all afternoon. Jenny had not once asked her mother for something to do. "The kid must be getting used to boredom,"

Janice said to herself.

"You guys ready to eat?" she yelled to the rest of the house.

A faint, "Any time, Mom," came from Todd's room. Nothing emanated from the other offspring.

"Todd, would you please find Jennifer and tell her it's nearly time to eat."

"Okay, Mom."

Janice went to the garage and picked out the cans she wanted from the makeshift shelving she had put together several years before for canned food storage. She kept rotating the cans as she used them so that the oldest food was always out in front.

"Jenny is asleep," reported Todd from the garage doorway. "You want me to wake her?"

"Yes, please," answered Janice. "She's got all night to sleep."

Janice returned to the kitchen with the cans. She took three potatoes from a dwindling supply in the cupboard and peeled them. She pumped up the camp stove and lit one burner. Then she sliced the potatoes and put them, along with some margarine, into a small skillet. This she placed on the burner. Later, when the potatoes were done, she would heat the beans in their own can with the lid removed. There would be no dirty pan to wash. The tuna would be eaten cold. She got out three paper plates and three plastic cups. The peaches would go into the cups. She had plastic knives, forks and spoons. Each person was allowed one set each day; then they were discarded. Nothing had to be washed.

"Ugh! What's that smell?" inquired a sleepy Jennifer as she came into the kitchen a few minutes later.

"Probably the tuna," answered her mother. "You like tuna, don't you?"

"I like *real* tuna I guess, not canned tuna," replied Jennifer.

Janice could see that they were going to get awfully tired of canned food. The kids were already complaining about it. She was tempted to tell them how lucky they were to have any food at all, but she decided it wouldn't make a big impression on them, so why bother. Tony had gone to work at the distribution center earlier. He always got something to eat there. Probably better food than he gets here, Janice thought.

The cat was at the back door complaining about his hunger pains. He was on a diet now consisting of one small can of moist cat food each day, plus some dry food from a sack. There didn't seem to be any leftovers from the table anymore. The cat didn't appear to be too pleased about the situation and vented his misery in shrill, nonstop wails.

Janice looked at Jennifer. "Better feed him, honey, or we'll never have any peace while we're eating."

"How do you like the book you borrowed from me, Todd?" she asked her son.

"It's pretty good, Mom," he answered. "Maybe a little too much lovey stuff and not enough action."

"Love is what makes the world go round," said Janice.

Todd looked at her and grimaced. "Are you and Tony in love?" he asked out of the blue.

The question stunned her. Was it so obvious, she wondered? "Well..." she began, without knowing what to say. Then she thought, why not be honest with Todd. He isn't a little kid anymore.

"I think so," she said finally. "It isn't that easy to answer. There have been so many tragic things happen lately. Under conditions like these, sometimes we misinterpret our feelings. Sometimes we think we feel things that aren't really true. Does that make any sense?"

"Sure," he said. "Makes a lot of sense."

Good old Todd, thought Janice. Always beyond his years in understanding.

"I hope you can get married someday," he said.

"You like Tony that well?" asked Janice.

"You bet. I think he's terrific."

"So do I," replied his mother, smiling.

"Who's terrific, Mickey the cat?" inquired Jennifer, coming back inside.

"Better wash if you touched him," said Janice.

"I didn't touch him, honest, Mom. I won't get cat dirt on my food," replied Jennifer. "Who's terrific?" she asked again.

"Oh, we were just talking," said Janice. "Nothing important."

"Then, I guess you mean Mickey's terrific," said Jennifer, with a note of finality in her voice.

The battery-operated clock in the dinette said 7:29 P.M. It was almost dark outside and Janice had pumped up and lit one of the Coleman lanterns. She wanted to work just a little more on her lecture before quitting for the day. Tony would be coming home soon, and then they would probably sit out on the patio, in the dark, and talk. That would give both of the kids a lantern in case they needed it for whatever they were doing. Right now they were playing a game of monopoly, so they needed only one source of light. She had just settled herself at the dinette table when she thought she heard people talking. It sounded like it was coming from out in front of the house. Maybe Tony was home already, talking to a neighbor. But she had a strange feeling—a feeling that something was wrong. She turned the lamp to "off." It sputtered, slowly dimmed, and finally went out. She went into the front room where she could hear through the open window. There were several young male voices talking quietly.

Janice froze. The radio had warned about teenage gangs going around, demanding money usually, or whatever they could get. Sometimes they were doing it in broad daylight. They had little to fear from the police, who were nearly impossible to contact because of telephone problems. And usually they were so busy there was no one to respond to a call. The radio said several people had been badly beaten by gang members within Janice's general area. One person had been killed, apparently for no reason. He had given them what money he had, but they shot him anyway and left him to die. Two women had been raped. She crept closer to the window to try to see who they were. She wished Tony were home.

The inside front door was open to let in the cool night air, but the screen door was locked. She knew that the screen door would not stop them for long, if it was a gang. They would simply cut the screen and let themselves in. She could see them cautiously approaching the house; there was still a trace of light in the western sky. She was sure they could not see her inside the dark house. They were quiet now. It was too dark to see each individual very well, but they looked young, perhaps 15 or 16 years old. Just about Todd's age. There were four of them that she could see. The one in front was carrying something. It was hard to see for sure, but it looked like a pistol.

Janice's heart was pounding so loudly she wondered if they might be able to hear it. She suddenly realized she was holding her breath. She exhaled and tried to breathe normally. She knew there was only one thing to do in order to protect herself and her children. She would have to play this just as rough as these half-grown hoodlums were playing it. They might not be adults, but they were dangerous. She thanked God she had had the foresight a few years ago to purchase a short barrel, 12-gauge shotgun. She kept it under her bed. She was not afraid of it and she knew how to use it. Her father had been an avid quail hunter when she was growing up. Janice was interested in any outdoor activity, so she begged him to take her when he went hunting. When she was a junior in high school, he bought her her own shotgun, and she had learned to use it almost as well as he. Those hunts were some of the greatest times she could remember having with her dad. He had probably wanted a son to hunt with, but she felt she had been a pretty good substitute.

She quickly and quietly moved to the front door, shut it and slammed the deadbolt into place. Then she ran to the bedroom and groped under the bed for the gun. It was wrapped in an old dress to keep dust out of it. She tore the cover off, pumped a shell from the magazine into the chamber and made sure the safety latch was on. She ran back to the front room where she could watch and hear. One of the gang had been saying something. It sounded like a little older voice. It had a heavy Spanish accent.

"Hey, who's in there? Why did you shut the door? We want to talk to you."

Janice said nothing. She was sweating and trying to control her breathing. She prayed that Jennifer and Todd would stay in the back of the house. What would she do if suddenly one of them appeared with the lantern wondering what was going on?

"Hey, you in there," the voice said. "We need some money. Give us money and we go away. We might break your door down and burn your house if you don't give us money." The words were slurred as if the person were drunk. Janice had been hoping they would simply give up and go away if she didn't respond. But now she could see the gun plainly in the hand of the one who was doing the speaking. They meant business.

"We might kill you if you don't open up," another heavily accented, but younger, voice said.

Janice decided she would have to say something. "I have no money," she said.

There was some surprised laughter from the group. "Oh, a lady, huh?" the leader said. "Where's your husband, lady? You open the door and come out of there or we might hurt you. But first we have some fun with you." More laughter.

Janice knew that time was running out. She had to do something now to take charge of the situation. She had to scare this bunch of thugs off. Either that or kill them if there was no other choice. She had absolutely no compunction about shooting at them if she had to. She knew it was either them or her and the kids. She would take her chances later with the authorities concerning what her "rights" might be, rather than let these punks have their way.

She remembered she had loaded her shotgun with magnum cartridges, four of them, containing triple-ought buckshot. She remembered because the gun salesman had made such a big issue out of the kind of cartridges she should have. He had told her these were best for riot control or self-defense.

One shot from a short barrel weapon loaded with this kind of round, he had said, could disable several people in a group if they were attacking. What she had to worry about was the guy with the pistol. He might shoot her before she could make her move. She was standing back from the window. He would probably shoot straight for the window. It could be a bluff, however. She had to try to scare them before she did anything more drastic.

She had no time to devise some kind of a plan. This would be off the top of her head. She drew a deep breath. Suddenly she lunged directly in front of the window. She drove the shotgun barrel at the window screen as hard as she could. It broke through easily, ripping a large hole. She knew this action was dangerous because she could be shot by the one with the pistol. She hoped the surprise of her move would freeze him. She unlatched the safety, pointed the gun skyward and pulled the trigger.

A simultaneous blinding flash and earthshaking explosion shattered the evening. A moment later her ears were ringing and she saw only a yellowish-white spot burned on her retinas. Then the spot began to fade as her sight returned. She pumped another shell into the chamber of the gun. Two of the human forms outside had broken ranks and were running. Two others were just standing there. The leader hadn't moved. She couldn't see where his pistol was pointed.

"Drop the gun or I'll shoot to kill," she screamed at the leader. The leader's companion was running away now too. The leader still stood there. Janice almost panicked. What in hell is he doing, she thought. Is he going to shoot?

"Drop the gun *now*, or your dead," she shouted.

The leader stood there a second more. "Don't shoot," he pleaded. He literally threw the pistol in her direction and ran.

Janice couldn't move. Her heart was pounding against her ribs. She was drenched with perspiration. There was a noise behind her. She turned. Todd was standing there in the doorway. The lantern that Jennifer was holding behind him silhouetted his body. How long had they been standing there?

Todd would have been a perfect target. Her body shuddered. Her knees buckled and she was, all of a sudden, sitting on the floor.

"Mom!" Todd yelled. "Are you all right?"

"Yes, I'm all right," she managed to choke out.

"Mama!" Jennifer screamed. Both children ran foreword and squatted beside her. Jennifer was hysterical. Janice took the child into her arms and tried to quiet her. In a minute her screaming changed into sobbing.

"Mom, are you hurt?" asked Todd. "What can I do?"

"I'm fine, dear, I'm fine. Please don't be frightened. Yes, there is one thing you can do," she said, holding Jennifer tightly to her. "Remember, I showed you about the shotgun? I showed you how to operate the safety catch. Please put the safety catch to the "on" position—very carefully. We don't want any accidents while we're waiting for Tony to come home."

SIXTEEN

Janice had just finished her lecture. A couple of students had come up to the front of the room to ask her several questions so they could clarify the notes they had just taken. These two will turn out to be among the best students in the class, Janice was thinking, after she had answered their questions. Why is it that the poorer students, the ones that really need help, never ask for any. It was the second week of the fall term and her third lecture in Zoology of Invertebrates. The lectures would be getting easier now. She always detested the first few lectures in a new class. "Getting to know you time," she called it. It got easier when she could remember the names of some of the students, and when they understood what they could expect from her.

Today she had talked about protozoans. It was one of her

favorite lectures in this course because nearly all of the students appeared to be actually interested. She had been telling them about how some of these tiny animals are parasites of humans. Malaria, leishmaniasis, African sleeping sickness, giardiasis, amoebic dysentery were only some of the human diseases caused by protozoans. Even the most disinterested students perked up when they discovered how the subjects of her lecture could harm them personally. She had noticed only one student sleeping out of a class of about 75. Usually there were two or three sleeping, and several more with a telltale glaze over their eyes, indicating they were not with her. The situation was especially difficult when she was explaining something complex, like the finer points of renal function in earthworms, or conjugation in paramecia. Tony, who also lectured in this course, had noticed the same phenomenon. So it wasn't just the way she presented the material.

A noise in the hall interrupted her reverie. Right now she had to get back to her office. In a few minutes she would have to be there for her office hour, a time when students could confer with her about almost anything.

The university had sustained severe damage in the earthquake. Almost miraculously, there had been no fires on campus. One building had collapsed, and several others had major structural damage and were condemned. Modular classrooms had been moved onto the campus. The science buildings had survived pretty well structurally, but the chemistry department had lost much of its glassware and glass-bottled reagents. Many laboratory courses had to be canceled. Some of biology's equipment had been damaged or destroyed; most supplies in the stock rooms had fallen from shelves and had broken or spilled. Many of the jars holding pickled specimens used for teaching had fallen and broken, much to the faculty's consternation. It would be difficult to replace these specimens with the totally inadequate budget situation at the university. It might be a long time before they could be replaced. Janice and Tony had also lost a few of their own specimens used in research, but these could be replaced by collecting more.

Utilities had been restored in many areas hit by the quake. By now, Janice's home had all of them intact. It was good to be able to use the toilet again and take a shower. Many schools had reopened. Jennifer's had reopened a week and a half ago. Todd's had finally reopened just two days ago. So, some things were getting back to normal. Other things would never be normal again after the heart-rendering loss of life and property. It would be years before the burned areas recovered, if ever.

Thousands of people had decided not to rebuild on the sites where their homes had been destroyed. They were abandoning their homesites and moving to new places, many of them completely out of California. Large numbers were moving to Oregon and Washington or eastward. Apparently some had concluded that it would be easier to face the ice and snow of the Middle West, rather than deal with the earthquakes and fires of the Far West. Ironically, the areas that had burned were among those that had housed some of the most affluent of the region's dwellers. Southern California would miss these big spenders and wealthy taxpayers. Tony was undecided what to do about his property. He, like many others, had discovered that his house insurance had been inadequate. He had not been careful enough in choosing his insurance coverage. It did not cover the entire cost of replacing what he had lost. He had been especially remiss in not having a list of his household possessions, along with photos of them locked away somewhere to show the insurance company. He would recover perhaps two thirds of his total losses. He was lucky to get anything: several insurance companies were on the edge of bankrupcy. He accepted the situation without comment. He just wasn't sure he wanted to rebuild, not in that particular place anyway.

Tony was still living with Janice and her children. Of course, he paid his share of household expenses, but he was still concerned about being a nuisance to them. However, they all seemed delighted that he was there. Especially Todd, who now had a "father." Janice was just as happy as Todd and did nothing to hide her feelings. Jennifer had moved back into her own bedroom, although with some reluctance at first. Every little aftershock of the earthquake frightened her, but she decided to be brave when they occurred. She didn't want to be like some of the crybabies at school that bawled sometimes, and seemed to be scared nearly all of the time. Besides, she could always run to her mother's bed in the middle of the night. Tony had moved his sleeping quarters to the front room, where there was a couch that folded out into a bed. It was a little inconvenient to have to unfold it at night and fold it back up in the morning, but it was the only arrangement he would accept. Janice had suggested putting Todd on the couch, and Tony taking Todd's room. Todd would have been happy to do it, but Tony would not hear of it.

Janice was a few minutes late getting back for her office hour. She had stopped to talk to a colleague briefly. Rarely did she have students coming in to see her anyway. Today, however, there was someone standing outside her office door. His back was turned, but the certain way that he stood plus the general outline of his backside told her, from the far end of the hall, that it was Dick Michaels, the department chairman. He turned just as she was about to greet him.

"Oh, Janice, there you are," he said.

"I'm sorry I'm a little late, Dick," she apologized.

"Late?" he questioned absentmindedly.

"For my office hour."

"Oh," he laughed. "Some people around here don't bother to show up at all. I guess I should get tough with them. Seems like there are more important things to do these days than getting after faculty members who abuse their office hours."

"I sure don't want your job," said Janice, smiling. "Not now; not with this budget situation that just seems to get worse every year."

"Yes, budget problems take at least half of my time now," Michaels answered. "Just between you and me, I'm sick of the whole thing. Thinking of retiring at the end of this year, in fact."

Janice acted surprised, although she had already heard rumors about it. She was slightly amused. Just between you and me, huh? she thought. That was typical of Michaels. He always liked to make you think that he was sharing something of his private life just with you. Probably the entire College of Science knew about it. Possibly the whole university. She motioned for him to sit down as she eased into the chair behind her desk.

"I'm getting too old to tolerate the constant hassle with money problems," he continued. "Maybe when I was younger it wouldn't have bothered me so much. I've had to tell too many good, part-time instructors that I couldn't afford them anymore. I can't forget the looks on their faces when I tell them."

Janice knew this was true. Old Michaels had his share of undesirable personality traits that made some people dislike and ridicule him. But he was a sympathetic, understanding and generous man. That much could not be taken away from him.

He went on. "Yes, we have problems here, don't we. It's terribly difficult to find money to hire new faculty, so when we lose someone, there may be no way to replace him. The faculty and staff haven't had a really significant pay increase in several years. That means our pay scale is low compared with other universities conquerable to us. And *that* means a morale problem among our people. We don't have adequate research funding. Travel money has all but dried up, so we spend money out of our pockets to attend scientific meetings." He stopped and grinned at Janice because of the absurdity of it all. Then he went on again.

"We don't have adequate supplies. We can't fix broken equipment and, of course, can't buy new equipment. It just seems like our entire program came to a dead stop, and then went into reverse. It's no fun running backwards, Janice. Not only this department, of course; every department in the university and every state university in California."

"When do you think it will get better?" she asked. He

looked at her as if he thought she were slightly naive.

"Janice," he said. "I don't know if it's going to get better. This state has dropped into a big hole. Some of it was bad luck, I guess. Certainly the earthquake and fires in this area, the recession, the end of the cold war and collapse of the aerospace industry. These we couldn't do much about. But some of it we did to ourselves. The passing of Proposition 13 a number of years ago, virtually freezing property taxes, was the first big mistake. It's been downhill ever since. Now it appears higher education will be getting a smaller percentage of the state budget every year.

"Another mistake has been letting so many immigrants into the state. We're supersaturated with them. It's costing us a fortune. Don't let any of these pro-immigrant people tell you it's good for us—like how much more they're paying in taxes than they cost us. I'm not saying a certain amount of immigration is bad. All I'm saying is that we've been overwhelmed with these people at a bad time. The illegals are the worst. They come here to get money, not to make the United States a better place to live. They taunt us by waving their Mexican flags in our faces, and then they're terribly hurt when we ask them where their allegiances are. When we don't love them as brothers, they call us racists. Is it surprising that we have mixed feelings about these people?

"Many illegals are paid under the table, and most of the taxes from those paid legally go to the Feds in Washington. California and its counties never see the major part of that money. Some of the people over in the College of Arts continually jawbone about how good it is to have all of these illegal—they call them undocumented—immigrants in California. Well, I guess its good for unscrupulous businesses. Illegals can be hired for next to nothing. It's certainly not good for the rest of us. Overcrowded county hospitals, millions driving without licenses or insurance, prisons overflowing, overburdened schools and teachers, gang fights and the killing of innocents, bankrupt welfare programs, wages kept so low that citizens can't make a decent living or even get a job. How can that be good for us?"

He stopped talking suddenly and looked at her. "I'm sorry, Janice, maybe you don't feel the way I do."

"Dick, I feel exactly the way you do. I couldn't agree with you more."

"Well, I didn't come to talk about Southern California's problems," he said. "It just seems like I've been so tied up that there was no way I could get a few moments to tell you how sorry I am about your two students who were lost in the fire. Actually, I didn't know about them until a couple of days after school began. I was on vacation, of course, when it happened. I guess everyone just figured that I knew. Finally, the Dean conferred his condolences and that was the first I had heard. So he told me as much as he knew about it. He said you had a close call yourself."

Janice filled him in on some of the details of what happened. "They think the fire was arson," Janice said finally, as a conclusion to the story. "They found a car hanging over the edge of a cliff on Mount Baldy road. The driver had been thrown out and they found him dead from a broken neck farther down the ravine. In the back seat of the car were several highway flares that matched the one they found where the fire started. It was partially burned but not entirely destroyed."

"Yes, I saw something about that in the newspaper," said Michaels. He was twirling his thumbs now, a habit that he appeared to have little control over. It happened when he was sitting and conversing with someone. Sometimes he would become conscious of what he was doing, and he would stop abruptly and look sheepish as if it were something to be ashamed of. Inevitably, it would begin again.

"You've been through a bad time, Janice," he said. "I'm sorry I didn't get to you sooner to talk about it. What about your chaparral research?"

"I haven't even thought about it," she admitted. "I'm not sure I can ever go back into the chaparral. I have a few hundred dollars left in my grant from the Forest Service. I'll probably just give the money back to them and write up some kind of report using what data I have already."

"You're that fearful of working in chaparral now?" asked Michaels.

"I don't think there is much fear involved," she answered. "It's just that I blame myself for what happened to Susan and Phil. I just can't face even the thought of chaparral without that terrible feeling of guilt coming over me."

"I think I know a little something about what you're faced with," said Michaels. "When my wife died years ago, I felt guilty about it. I felt there was something I could have done to prevent her dying. Perhaps I didn't get her to the hospital quickly enough. Finally, when I started thinking more rationally again, I decided I did about what anyone else would have done. Maybe that's all that can be expected. These insights that we have long after something terrible has happened don't help us much right away. I hope you will gradually come to the conclusion that you need to stop blaming yourself."

"But what I did was so dumb," Janet murmured.

"All of us do dumb things," answered Michaels. "Most of the time we get away with them; sometimes we don't and then we get hurt. I don't know. Maybe it's a matter of luck. Have you talked to their parents?"

"I haven't had the courage yet," admitted Janice. "I want to but…" Her face contorted. She couldn't say more.

"Pretty soon you'll be able to, Janice. It just takes time. I think it may help you when you can do it. I hope they are understanding people," he said.

He rose from his chair and, totally out of character for him, he took her hand. He very rarely touched anyone if it wasn't necessary. "Is there anything I can do to help, Janice?" he asked.

"No," she said, "but thank you." He released her hand. She also rose from her chair.

"Your house came through the earthquake pretty well according to Tony," Michaels said. "I'm happy for you on that account anyway. I guess you knew my condo was destroyed. I was on vacation. Lost everything except what I had with me."

Janice had not heard.

"No, I didn't know," she said. "I'm awfully sorry."

"Thank you. I guess we all lost something."

"Where are you living?" she asked.

"Oh, I moved in with an old friend. We've known each other for at least 40 years. It's a temporary arrangement I guess, but it's almost impossible to find an apartment. Maybe he'll let me stay there until I retire. Then I'll probably leave the area. He paused. Well, I have to go, Janice. Remember, call me if you need anything."

Maybe Michaels was right, Janice thought after he left. Maybe it will be better after I talk to Susan's and Phil's folks. I can get it off my chest then. I think I'll try to call them later this afternoon or tonight and find out if they even want to see me. Maybe they don't. Maybe they will be hostile. Well, there's one way to find out.

SEVENTEEN

It was just after 3:30 P.M. Janice had been working on a departmental committee assignment much of the afternoon. She normally hated committee work since she considered much of it boring, and many times one or two people ended up doing most of the work. But this committee was not so bad. All the members were competent, knew what they had to do and came to meetings with their work completed. She had been pleased to find herself within such a competent group.

Tony would be winding up his lecture about now and his students would be getting a little restless in anticipation of 3:50, when they were free. Then he would get together the things he wanted to take home and come by her office to see if she was ready to leave. Or, more likely, he would phone first from his office since she might be tied up with a student or something. When he came through her office door, he would close it behind him. She would get up from her desk. He would put down his briefcase and whatever else he was carrying, and they would kiss tenderly. Then she would gather up the things she wanted to take home and they would leave.

Tender seemed to be the perfect word to describe their feelings about each other. She was surprised and perhaps a little unsettled by the total lack of passion so far. Tony hadn't suggested in either words or actions that he needed some kind of physical lovemaking. Three or four tender kisses a day was about the extent of it. But then, she was surprised by her own total lack of need also. The fire and loss of Susan and Phil seemed to have destroyed her physical desires. She hadn't even daydreamed about making love since that fatal day. Perhaps Tony understood how she felt and would not push her. She was still on uncertain ground emotionally, and he would not press her into anything until she got back to normal. But it was very strange how they had not even discussed their feelings. She didn't want to bring it up because she wasn't certain how Tony felt, and anyway, she was old fashion enough to feel it was the man's place to initiate such things. She knew she was deeply in love with Tony, and she was almost sure he felt the same about her, but she needed to be told. Maybe he didn't really love her and could not lie to her, so he said nothing. But she could not believe this explanation. It must be that he didn't want to press her now; or perhaps, manlike, he didn't realize that she needed confirmation. She might have to put her old fashioned inhibitions aside and let him know how she felt.

But she would not do it yet. It might turn into a disastrous rejection for her and she was not ready for anything like that. For now she was happy enough with things the way they were, even if there was some uncertainty. Another possibility had just lately occurred to her. Perhaps he didn't know yet how he felt and was waiting to get a clearer perception of his emotions. His kisses told her this probably wasn't the answer either. And his eyes told her even more. He was in love with her all right, and knew it. But poor, quiet Tony didn't know how to say the words. Yes, that must be it. She would probably have to help him.

Earlier in the afternoon Janice had finally screwed up enough courage to call the phone number of Susan's parents. She had obtained the number from the university's Records Office. Half-hoping no one would answer, she had removed the receiver, listened for the dial tone and pressed the sequence of buttons. She had waited through four rings. Heaving an uncertain sigh of relief, she was ready to hang up when the receiver at the other end was lifted and a woman said "hello." Janice nearly panicked and choked out a weak "hello." The woman apparently didn't hear her and said, louder this time, "hello, who is this?" The voice had a weak Asian accent.

"Mrs. Shigawa?" inquired Janice.

"Yes," the voice said. Janice calmed down a little and awkwardly explained who she was and what she wanted. She asked Mrs. Shigawa if she and her husband were available sometime on Saturday. Janice would like to talk to them.

Mrs. Shigawa hesitated for a long moment. Janice held her breath. Finally Mrs. Shigawa said she would have to talk with her husband. He would call Janice back if she would leave her number. Janice gave her both the office number and her home number. She thanked Mrs. Shigawa and hung up. She was shaking when it was over. She wondered if Mr. Shigawa would call back.

Ten minutes later when her shaking spasm was fairly well under control, she had resolutely picked up the phone receiver once again and punched in the numbers that Records had given her for Phil's home. She needed to get this business over with as quickly as possible. The phone rang once and there was a young woman's voice on the line.

"Mrs. Granger?" asked Janice.

"This is Florence," the voice had said. "My mother is out but perhaps I can help you."

Janice again went through the awkward explanation and waited for the reaction.

"I'm really glad you called, Dr. Ballard. I know my mother would like to talk to you, and I'd like to also if you don't mind. By the way, I'm Phil's older sister."

Janice had made an appointment for Sunday afternoon since Florence had assured her that it would be a convenient time. Phil's father was away working and didn't get home very often, so he wouldn't be available.

Janice heaved a great sigh of relief after she hung up. Now the die was cast. She would at least get to talk with Phil's family, and possibly with Susan's. She felt she was doing what was right regardless of how it all came out. She had instinctively liked Phil's sister over the phone. She had sounded so positive and upbeat in spite of the subject they had discussed. Janice knew she was going to like this girl when they met. She might not have the same feelings for Mrs. Shigawa.

The phone on Janice's desk rang. It was undoubtedly Tony, but she answered with the usual, "Biology Department."

"Hi there," Tony's voice said. "Is the Biology Department ready to go home?"

"Don't get smart with me, mister," laughed Janice. "I don't go so much for wise guys."

"Does that mean you're going to walk home? I'm not sure I'll let you ride in *my* car with that attitude."

"And I'm not sure I'll let you come to *my* house if that's the way you're going to be."

Tony laughed his quiet, gentle laugh. "See you in a minute," he said. Almost exactly one minute later he appeared in her doorway. She had everything she was taking home together in a pile. It was a large pile. "Guess what," she said.

"You're moving out of your office?" Tony was looking at the pile and grinning.

"I called Susan's mother and Phil's big sister today. I'm going to see Phil's family on Sunday if I can borrow your car, and maybe Susan's parents on Saturday, if Mr. Shigawa calls back. I finally feel ready to talk to them. Isn't that wonderful? But I'm so scared, Tony. No, I'm not scared. I'm totally terrified!"

"Janice, you'll be fine. Want me to go with you?"

"No, Tony. This is my problem. I have to do it alone."

"If you say so." He closed the office door and came toward her. They embraced. She closed her eyes and tilted her head upward so that her lips could more easily meet his. When nothing happened, she opened her eyes again inquiringly.

"I want to tell you something, Janice," he said. "I've been wanting to for some time. I've kept putting it off."

"Yes?" she said. She could feel her heart pounding in her chest. He was going to tell her that he wasn't in love with her, that he had tried but it was simply no use.

"It's just that…Well, that I love you so much. I hope that is okay with you." He looked at her as if he half-expected her to be angry or something.

She just said, "Oh, Tony," and let her kisses be the answer.

About two minutes later she said, "There, does that tell you whether it's okay with me?"

"I guess so," he said. "But I mean I really want you to be my wife. I'm not so hot at the idea of just living together without marrying."

She looked at him, her lips showing the barest traces of a sarcastic smile.

"Oh, I know we already have been," he said. "But that's different. Do you think enough of me to consider marrying me?" He had such an uncertain, worried look on his face that she simply could not help laughing.

"Tony, is this a proposal?" she asked.

"Yes, I guess it is. I know I don't have much to offer you. I don't even have a house right now," he said with a frown.

"Tony, *I* have a house, *you* have a car. I guess we really need each other. My answer is yes before you can change your mind."

His frown transformed into a rapturous smile. "I love you," he said.

"And I love you just as much," was the reply.

They decided on the way home not to keep it a secret from

Todd and Jenny. There was no reason to. They felt sure of their own feelings. The only problem might be with one of the children. Janice simply could not imagine a negative reaction from Todd. He would be ecstatic about their marriage. He had told her some time ago that he hoped they could get married some day. Jennifer might be a different matter. Janice just didn't know how her daughter would react. Would there be some jealousy? Would Jennifer suddenly change her mind about Tony and decide that he was taking her mother from her? It was certainly a possibility, but waiting to tell her didn't appear to hold any advantages.

As they approached Janice's house, they noticed a car out in front. "Wonder who that could be?" Janice mused. "Do you recognize the car, Tony?"

"Totally strange to me," he said. "Maybe somebody visiting across the street."

"Maybe," she agreed. Tony parked in the driveway.

"Will you help me with some of this stuff, please, Tony?" Janice asked. "I don't think I can carry it all."

"Take what you can. I'll grab the rest," he said. Janice struggled to open the front door of her home with both arms loaded. Finally she got the knob turned just enough to release the latch, and the door swung open. She saw Todd across the room sitting upright, rather awkwardly, in the big reclining chair in the corner.

"Todd, could you help me with a few of these things?" she said.

Out of the corner of her eye, on the other side of the room, Janice noticed a figure rising to its feet. She turned her head, did a quick take and murmured, "hello," giving the figure a half-smile. The next moment she froze, then turned her entire body to face the figure.

"Scott, what are you doing here?" she gasped. Tony had just come in the door. He stopped when he saw Janice standing there staring, with an incredulous look on her face. He looked at the stranger across the room, then back to Janice.

"What is it, Janice?" he said.

"Tony, this is Todd's father," she finally managed to blurt out. "His name is Scott," she added.

Tony looked again at the man. He advanced slowly toward him and they shook hands.

"Let me have some of that stuff you're carrying, Janice," Tony offered. He took several things from Janice and disappeared with them into the back of the house. He judged that it would be better if he were not present in the front room.

Scott had sat down again. Janice laid the rest of what she was carrying down on one end of the sofa and sat down on the other end. She noticed she was having trouble getting her breath. She gave Scott a long, careful scrutiny. He was wearing faded jeans and tennis shoes. She couldn't see that he had changed much. Perhaps 15 or 20 pounds heavier, that was about all. From the look on his face, it was obvious he was enjoying her consternation and surprise. This made her angry. He had said nothing yet.

Finally, she broke the silence. "What do you want?" she asked, looking straight at him.

"I just wondered how you and Todd were doing," he said. Janice looked over at Todd, who was still sitting uncomfortably in his chair, seemingly not knowing what to make of the situation.

"Todd, would you mind leaving us alone a few minutes," Janice said. "We want to talk."

"Sure, Mom, I've got some homework." He got up and left the room.

"Maybe you should have let him stay, Janice," Scott said. "It wouldn't have hurt any."

"No, I want to know what you're up to."

"I'm not up to anything, Janice." he said. "I just came to see how everything is."

"You've been worried about us, have you?" replied Janice sarcastically. "It's taken you a long time to decide what to do about it. How did you find us?"

"Oh, it's not hard to find anybody if you really want to. All you need is a name. I knew you were here in Southern

California. After the earthquake and fire, I got a little concerned and decided to find out if you were all right."

"Why didn't you just call my folks?"

"I wanted to see for myself. After all, I've never even seen Todd before."

"Yeah, that's the enigma, I guess," said Janice. "You've never been concerned enough before to even take a look at your son, let alone helping to support him. Now, suddenly, you're worried. I guess I'm suspicious."

"You don't have to be," he said. "I have no ulterior motive. I was curious as well as concerned. You're looking pretty good, Janice. Aren't you going to ask anything about me?"

"I don't care anything about you," she answered.

"Well, I'm teaching in a community college up in Oakland," he said. "I'm married and my wife works for a bank. We don't have any children. I've changed a lot, Janice. I've settled down. I'm not the same person." Janice did nothing to hide her skepticism, but didn't say anything.

"Who's the guy with you?" he asked. "I was led to believe you were still single."

"He's just a friend," replied Janice. "His house was destroyed in the fire and he's been staying with us because he has no place else to go."

"That's pretty nice of you," he said. Janice stared at him, but could not decide whether he was implying something more than what his statement said. His face was inscrutable. In any event, she didn't care. They looked at each other for a few unsure moments.

Finally he said, "Well, I guess it's time to go. I'm sorry if I startled you by coming here, Janice. But I'm glad I got a chance to see Todd. Looks like you've done a good job raising him. I understand you have a daughter too."

"Jennifer," replied Janice.

"That's nice," he said. He rose, walked toward her and extended his hand. She also rose. She wasn't sure if she wanted to take it, but she finally did.

"You've got a nice place here," he said. "Have to drive

back to Oakland tomorrow. It was nice seeing you again, Janice."

Janice said nothing.

He paused a moment, then went to the front door, opened it, walked out and closed it behind him. Janice never moved from the spot where she was standing. Finally, she went to the front window as he was driving away. Tony stuck his head around the corner of the hall.

"All clear?" he asked.

"Yes, he's gone, Tony. What do you suppose he wanted? Did you hear what he said?" Tony looked a little sheepish.

"I'll have to admit I did," he said. "I was afraid to leave you alone with him. I hope you'll forgive me for listening."

"No, I'm glad you did. Did you believe him?"

"Oh, I don't know, Janice. How can I tell? You know him. Didn't you believe him?"

"I don't know either. He does appear to be somewhat different. I wonder what he told Todd?"

"Ask Todd," suggested Tony.

"What a time for him to show up and upset everyone," lamented Janice. "Just when we are making some happy plans, this creep appears and spoils everything. Do you suppose he'll try to influence Todd in some way? Is that what he wants?"

"I think you're making too much of it, Janice. I don't know how he could do very much influencing when he is in Oakland and Todd is here. Besides, Todd is a pretty steady, sensible kid. I don't think he'll fall for anything like that."

Tony took her hand. "Does this, for any reason, change our plans?" he asked.

Janice kissed him. "Of course not," she said. "I want to talk to Todd first to see what I can find out. Then we'll eat dinner and tell the kids. Okay?"

"Okay by me." He squeezed her hand tightly.

EIGHTEEN

The phone call had come about 8:00 P.M. that same evening. Dinner was over, the dishes were done, and Janice had had her talk with her son. Todd reported nothing extraordinary about the meeting with his father. He said they just talked about how Todd liked school, whether he had any hobbies, and that sort of thing. Todd didn't seem to take his father's visit very seriously. Still….During dinner, Tony and Janice had told the children their news. As expected, Todd simply beamed when he heard it. He couldn't have been happier. Jennifer took it with very little emotion. Janice was watching her daughter closely and she appeared to be bewildered more than anything else. Apparently, the possibility of such a thing had never entered her mind. But at least she did not seem to be unhappy about the news.

The phone call had been from Mr. Shigawa. He wanted to go over the details of the meeting with Janice, even though Janice had carefully explained the purpose of it to Mrs. Shigawa. His formal, business like manner puzzled and frightened Janice a little. She had been hoping for a more friendly reaction. But at least he had said that he and his wife would be willing to talk to her. He suggested three o'clock Saturday afternoon.

Now it was Saturday, 2:46 P.M. by Janice's watch. She had borrowed Tony's car, taken Interstate 10 to Santa Monica and was looking for the street where the Shigawas lived. There it was just ahead. "Take a right turn," Mr. Shigawa had told her, "and look for our house number about a block and a half farther up the street." Janice was a little early. Before going any farther, she decided to park on the shady side of the street and wait about ten more minutes. It was exactly what she had hoped wouldn't happen. She had wanted to find the place right on time, and not have to sit around cooling her heels and thinking. The wait would only make her more nervous, and she was already having serious doubts. There was just time to have a cigarette.

She took a cigarette from the pack in her purse and lit it with the lighter in Tony's car. She had never used his ash tray since Tony was a non-smoker and might not be too keen about having his ash tray full of cigarette butts. She had looked inside the ash tray once and decided that it had probably never been used by anyone. Filthy habit, she thought to herself. How did I ever get hooked? She had already promised herself she would quit smoking before marrying Tony. He had never said anything, but she could see his distaste for the habit.

She sat and thought about her doubts concerning this meeting with the Shigawas. The doubts had begun the same afternoon she had called Mrs. Shigawa. The lady had sounded so cold and aloof. Mr. Shigawa had seemed a little more congenial, but only in a business-like way. He was probably used to making business calls over the phone and had developed the proper tone and manner. Anyway, why should they be pleased about it? They probably weren't looking forward to it any more than she was. On the other hand, if she were them, wouldn't she be curious about the details of the disaster? Wouldn't she want to know everything that happened that day? She was reasonably certain that she would.

The door was opened by a rather short, square faced oriental man, perhaps in his early fifties. His hair was beginning to gray.

"Mr. Shigawa?" asked Janice.

"Yes," he said, bowing slightly. "You must be Dr. Ballard. Please come in." He did not offer to shake her hand.

He led her into a rather dimly lit room. There was a mixture of Japanese and American decor in the room. A pretty oriental woman was standing there.

"Dr. Ballard, this is Mrs. Shigawa," he said. The lady also bowed slightly and greeted Janice but did not extend her hand.

"Please sit down," she said.

Later, Janice tried to be objective about the meeting. Had it accomplished anything? The Shigawas were totally inscrutable. They listened to her story without a trace of emotion. They had only two or three questions to ask her. She had explained in exact detail what had happened that day, making no attempt to lessen her own responsibility for the tragedy. They had said nothing, neither trying to exonerate her from some of that responsibility nor attempting to implicate her further. It was like a meeting of the dead. Getting no emotion from them, she felt none and gave none. It was as if she had conveyed a message that had been carefully and hopefully crafted to create a response—any response, positive or negative, as long as there was some communication—only to find that communication was not possible.

She left them as she had come. Slight bows from each but no physical contact. They thanked her for coming, but without a trace of understanding or compassion. Before getting back on the Interstate, she stopped in the parking lot of a supermarket she had passed on the way in. She parked as far away from the other cars as possible. She took another cigarette from the pack in her purse, smoked it and cried.

When Janice got back home, Tony could see she had been crying. He caught her and wrapped his arms around her. "Didn't go so good, huh sweetheart?" he said.

"Oh Tony, it was awful. I don't know why I did it. I didn't realize it was going to get so painful. And they didn't seem to care. It just seemed like they wanted to get it over with and get me out of their house. Just a duty that they had to perform. I don't know if they cared about what happened that day. I thought I was going to help them and myself. Maybe I just made it worse for all of us."

He hugged her tightly and she clung to him. "Maybe it's just a cultural difference, Janice. Maybe that's the correct way for them to react. Something we don't understand. Anyway, I think you did the right thing, and I also think that you will come to the same conclusion in time when some of the pain wears off. It just takes time, honey. Time cures nearly everything."

"I don't know if I can go through with another meeting tomorrow," she said. "I'm not sure I can face it. Maybe I should just call Phil's family and tell them I can't make it."

"I think that's the worse thing you could do, Janice. Didn't you tell me that Phil's sister indicated over the phone that she was looking forward to talking to you? I suspect your experience tomorrow will be totally different. I don't think it's right for you to cancel out if they are really looking forward to seeing you."

"I suppose you're right, she said. "I just can hardly bear the pain. It's so hard for me. I wish I could be like you. You never seem to let tragedy get to you. The loss of your home didn't seem to affect you. It was just like you could brush it off. Where do you get courage like that?"

"Listen, Janice, you're comparing two entirely different things. Losing one's house is nothing like what has happened to you. I don't have any more courage than you do. You are just as gutsy as anybody I know, and don't you forget it." He massaged her neck and back as he was talking, trying to get her to relax a little.

"Okay, Tony, I'll go talk to them tomorrow. If you say it's right, then it has to be right."

He groaned. "Don't put me on a pedestal I have no business occupying. I can be just as wrong as anybody. But I think this is right. And what's more important, I think that *you* think it's right." He kissed her forehead, and then her lips.

That night after the kids were in bed and after Tony had once again transformed the front room sofa into his own bed and retired, Janice quietly went to him and said, "I want to be with you tonight. Would you be willing to do this for me?" He answered without uttering a single word. She led him to her bedroom and together they closed the door.

The house was in a rather run-down area of south Ontario. Janice looked at it carefully as she was getting out of the car. It didn't look like a house; it looked more like a small church. There was something that resembled a steeple in front. A rather neglected looking, 10 or 12 year-old Ford occupied the driveway. There didn't appear to be a doorbell, so Janice knocked. The door was opened by a tall, rather plain looking girl in her middle twenties. She looked something like Phil but had brown hair and lacked his sharp features. Her soft brown eyes attracted Janice immediately.

"Dr. Ballard," she said. "How nice of you to come and see us." She extended her hand to Janice. "I'm Florence. We talked on the phone."

Janice was led into a huge room that must have taken up most of the building. The front part of the room contained a sofa and three easy chairs, all unmatched and with a well used and worn look to them. Farther back was a large dining table painted blue. It was surrounded by eight wooden chairs of two varieties. Four of them were painted blue and did not quite match the color of the table. The other four were yellow. To one side of the room was the kitchen with a battered looking refrigerator and a somewhat better looking cooking range. In the back of the room were several beds, all neatly made. The house appeared to be clean and livable. A whole house in one room, thought Janice.

A door in the back of the room opened and a lady, older than Janice, with bright red hair appeared.

"Dr. Ballard, this is my mother," Florence said. The lady smiled and extended her hand.

"How do you do, Mrs. Granger," said Janice.

"Please call me Nancy," said the lady.

"I will if both of you call me Janice," replied Janice. "I'm uncomfortable with too much formality." They sat down on the worn furniture in the "living room" area of the house.

With no further preliminaries, Janice plunged into the subject of her visit. She had one thing only in mind: to get it over with. She wanted to tell these people what happened that awful day and bear the consequences, whatever they might be. Perhaps the two would be understanding, but even their wrath would be better than the non-reaction which she had experienced the previous day.

Florence and her mother listened spellbound as Janice worked her way through the tragedy. There were many questions and Janice did her best to answer them fully and truthfully. She tried to contain the emotion that began flooding through her as the story unfolded. Near the end she could contain the flood no longer and she struggled to get the words out. Florence got out of her chair and sat down on the sofa beside Janice. She took Janice's hand in both of hers. Tears were running down her cheeks. Janice could go no further. Silent sobs shook her body. All three women were crying now. When Janice finally got control again she said, "I'm so terribly sorry. So much of it was my fault. He was such a fine young man. I know you can never forgive me and I never can forgive myself for what happened."

Mrs. Granger looked up, drying her eyes. "Janice, you must never say anything like that again. We are not blaming you for what happened and we never will. It's been hard for us, but I can see now how much harder it's been for you. You must not feel responsible for this. It just happened and we accept it that way." Turning to her daughter, she said, "Florence, if you would put on the coffee pot, perhaps we could persuade Janice to stay and have coffee and cookies with us. I just baked this morning."

Janice stayed a full two hours. They talked about their lives and their dreams. It was obvious to Janice that money was scarce in this household. Yet it didn't seem to bother them that they didn't have money or the conveniences. Nancy worked as a clerk in a department store. She probably makes very little money, Janice thought to herself. Florence worked part-time several evenings a week as a waitress; but primarily, she took care of the four younger children in the family. She was their "mother" during the daytime when their real mother worked to make a living. Most of Florence's income, what there was of it, probably also went to the family, guessed Janice. Apparently the father was off somewhere and contributed little to the household, other than sperm to make more children.

Finally, Janice decided, reluctantly, that she should be going. Tony and the kids would be wondering about her. These were lovable people and Janice already felt a large, warm spot in her heart for them, even in such a short time.

As they were saying good-bye at the front door, Florence took Janice's hand once again and said, "Janice, thank you for coming to see us. It means so much, especially to Mom. It must have been very difficult for you to come. I hope we'll see each other again."

Janice squeezed her hand and replied, "We'll make it a point to." All three hugged and held each other tightly for a moment before Janice departed.

NINETEEN

Thanksgiving and Christmas had come and gone. Thanksgiving had been a joyous occasion. Janice had invited Nancy and Florence Granger and the four younger children over to her house. It was quite a crowd to serve for dinner, but she managed to accommodate everyone by using card tables and improvised seating. One of Nancy's daughters was just a year younger than Todd. It was obvious that Todd was attracted to her. Janice was amused since she had never known Todd to show much interest in girls. Tony grasped the situation also and winked at Janice.

"Hormones starting to take control," he suggested.

"Not yet I hope," she had replied. Jennifer had taken charge of the two younger children, a boy and a girl. She loved to have this kind of responsibility, and they played together all afternoon.

Christmas was a little different. Janice had never particularly liked Christmas, at least not since she was in her late teens. She regarded it as mostly a money making venture for retailers, and the whole thing turned her off. It often began late in October, even before Halloween, when Christmas decorations started to appear in stores. It just seemed to Janice that it went on and on, and she was already sick of it by early December. She was always exceedingly happy to see the new year roll around. This Christmas had been special, however, since Janice had received a diamond from Tony, and they were beginning to make plans for the wedding. It would be a small affair, probably just Tony's and Janice's parents and a few friends. Janice wondered if Tony would feel cheated by not having a more elaborate ceremony since it was his first. But he seemed relieved when, after some discussion, they settled on something very simple, probably right in Janice's home.

Tony had finally received his house insurance money, and the loan had been paid off. He had made no plans to rebuild his home. Janice had brought the subject up once or twice just to get a little better grasp of the situation, but he had appeared to be totally undecided at the time. More recently, he had told her that he simply had bad feelings about rebuilding there, and would probably end up trying to sell the lot unless she particularly wanted him to rebuild in that spot. The problem was that no one was buying land in the areas that had burned. Very few of the other people who had lost their homes were rebuilding either, so the land values had fallen tremendously. Both felt that Janice's house was too small for them, and it had the inconvenience of only one bathroom. They decided to look elsewhere for a house as soon as summer arrived and the university term was concluded. Janice would be pleased to have the children in a different school district, although every district was suffering from lack of money.

Janice had purchased an older subcompact sedan so she could have transportation when Tony was researching at the beach. She had not resumed work on any of her research projects since the fire. She knew she would never do anything more on the chaparral project, so she had returned to the Forest Service what little money there was remaining in her grant. She also had written up a short report of her unfinished results and submitted it with the money. She still had plans to return to her other research projects, but for some reason it was difficult. She kept postponing any further effort, and she didn't understand why. Tony told her she should just wait until she was ready. After all, no one was pushing her since she had no grant support now. She felt that her teaching responsibilities were heavy enough presently without having other things to do.

Nothing had changed at the university. The budget crunch was getting no better. It could very easily get even worse. Janice and Tony were working harder now setting up laboratory exercises that had previously been prepared by graduate students, who had occupied teaching assistant positions. Most of these positions were a thing of the past. There was no money to support them. Graduate students had to find some other way to earn enough money to get through school. Several of them had dropped out.

Late in January, Janice had received a letter from Dr. Bradley Figgens, one of her former classmates at Berkeley. Brad had obtained his degree when Janice did, and had gone to Texas A&M on a post-doctorate appointment. She had lost track of him after that, but his letter indicated that three years after going to Texas, he had obtained a tenure-track position at the University of Florida. She had had a glimpse of him once or twice at national entomological meetings that she attended, but had not had the chance to talk to him. Apparently, he had kept better track of her.

His letter had indicated that there was an opening for an entomologist to do some research in the tropics of Central America, and perhaps later in South America as well. He had heard about some of the problems the universities were having in California, and wondered whether she might be interested in applying for the job. He was a member of the committee in charge of searching for applicants.

At first Janice put the thought out of her mind. After all, she was about to get married. She would phone Brad and tell him the situation. She did not mention the opportunity to Tony. It was out of the question so why bother him with it. But she found that it had been difficult to suppress the matter in spite of all the objections she could think of. She would dearly love to get out of this place for many reasons; but, of course, she didn't know how Tony would feel about it. His reluctance to rebuild his home led her to speculate that he might not have major objections. Somehow, she felt that he, too, was becoming disenchanted with Southern California. But still, she could not ask Tony to uproot himself just to follow her.

The third day after having received the letter she decided, in fairness to Brad, to phone him and explain the circumstances. She would also try to find out more about the position just to satisfy herself that it was not something she wanted or would qualify for. Unfortunately, it turned out to be exactly what she thought she would like, and Brad had indicated that he thought she was highly qualified. Otherwise, he would not have written to her. He told her to think it over. She had a couple of weeks to apply.

Once again she attempted to push the matter to the farthest recesses of her mind. She would simply let the application time expire, and then the problem would resolve itself.

Two days later, Tony and she had been talking at the dinner table after the two children had excused themselves. Somehow the conversation got turned around to the subject of opportunities. Tony had said something about always taking advantage of opportunities when they came along, and didn't she agree with that. She had replied that it was nice to take advantage of opportunities, but that sometimes it was not possible to do so. She must have had a strange look on her face because Tony became silent and peered at her for a moment.

He had said, "Janice, I'm getting to know you pretty well. Why don't you tell me about it."

She was flabbergasted. How could Tony know? But she

tried not to show her surprise.

"About what?" she asked.

"About whatever it is you're hiding from me," he had said.

She had laughed. "Can you actually read me so easily?"

He grinned at her. "It's not some other man, is it?"

She chided him with her eyes. "I may as well come clean," she said. "I can see you have ESP."

"Not at all," he had said. "Simply getting to know the one I love."

Then she told him about the letter from Brad Figgins. "Tell me all about it," he had said.

"Well, there's a new position that has been created for an entomologist to work in Central America, although later they want to expand the work into South America. It has to do with the diversity of tropical species problem that we've heard so much about the last few years."

"Oh, you mean trying to determine how many species of animals and plants there are in tropical forests before the forests have all been cut down or burned. Yes, that's terribly vital work that needs to be done."

"Not only how many species, but something about their biology and economic value. And, of course, they hope to save what they can of these forests *before* they're destroyed. I'd probably have only a slight chance of landing the position," continued Janice. "There are undoubtedly some good applicants. Work like that would appeal to many people."

"I think you should apply, Janice. What harm can it do? I know you're not terribly happy here anymore. Tell me some of the details. I'm interested."

"Well, it's a tenure track position with the University of Florida at Gainesville, but apparently the Federal Government is funding part of it. Most of it would be field collecting and studying the ecology of some of the unknown and little-known insects in the American tropics. We know virtually nothing about these insects. We don't even have a good idea about how many species there are—probably millions. Many of them have become extinct because so much of the tropical forest has already been destroyed. There are various reasons for our need to know more about them. The economic reason is that they probably contain chemicals in their bodies that might be useful to us, just like some plants do."

"Yes," said Tony. "Some chemicals from certain marine invertebrate animals are already being used in medicine. What about the tropical rainy season?"

"The rainy season in the tropics lasts several months," answered Janice. "During these months the person would be stationed at Gainesville. But anyway, suppose I got lucky and landed the appointment. You have your teaching position here and your research. I can't ask you to uproot yourself and follow me. And if you think I'd leave you here, you had better think again," she added, with a playful glint in her eye.

"Janice, there are other jobs. I'm not that crazy about staying here. Perhaps I could just help you in your work for a while. Something would probably turn up for me sooner or later."

"I don't want to do that, Tony. Suppose nothing did turn up. Jobs aren't that easy to find. I'd feel very guilty about taking you away from what you have here. You might start hating me for doing that to you."

"Yes, sweetheart, I'm sure I would," said Tony, smiling. "Why don't you go ahead and apply. You say you probably won't get the appointment, and in that case there's no problem. In the event that you did happen to get it, we could discuss it some more. You could still turn it down at that point. But we could also look into the possibilities for me. What about the kids? Have you thought about them?

"I haven't allowed myself much time to think about any aspect of this thing," she had said, "it just seems so impossible." The statement was not entirely true. She *had* given some thought to how the children would be affected. In spite of her efforts to put the matter aside, it had occupied some of her thoughts.

In the end, she had submitted her application barely in time to meet the deadline. Now, three weeks later, she had heard nothing except that the application had been received in Florida.

Janice glanced at her watch. It was five minutes after twelve. She and Tony had eaten their paper-bag lunches in her office a little earlier. Her office boasted a little more space than his, so this was where they usually came together for whatever purpose. She had a lecture to give in fifty-five minutes, and now she hoped there would be no interruptions so that she could study her notes in preparation for her presentation.

As if willfully plotting to counteract her wishes, the phone rang. Janice picked up the receiver and said, "Biology Department."

"Janice?" the voice asked.

"Speaking," she said.

"Hi, this is Brad Figgins. How are you, Janice?"

"Brad! I'm fine. How's yourself?"

"Oh, can't complain, I guess. Overworked and underpaid as the saying goes. I was delighted to receive your application for the tropics position. I was afraid you might have decided not to apply. We got a tub-full of applications. But, as usual, many of the applicants don't qualify, or they don't have the background we're looking for, or there's some other problem."

"Any idea yet how far down the tub I am, Brad? I suppose I sank to the bottom right away."

"That's what I called about," Brad answered. "I am overjoyed to report that you are on the short list, Janice. And my specific reason for calling is to ask you to visit us and give us a seminar. At our expense, of course. Think you could do that?" Janice hesitated for a long moment.

"Janice? Anything wrong?"

"No, Brad. I was just considering," said Janice. "When would this seminar have to be?"

"Well, next week or the early part of the week after, whichever is more convenient. You don't sound very excited, Janice. I hope that nothing has come up to change your mind."

"No, Brad, nothing at all. That is; nothing you don't know about."

"Oh, you mean your imminent marriage plans. Yes, that must be a tough problem for you. I sure hope you can come to some agreement with your fiancé in case things go in your favor concerning the job opening. Personally, I think you have an excellent chance for this position. And, you know, Janice, I certainly can't make any promises, but there could very well be an associate position of some kind later on to go with the one you have applied for. We would love to have a husband and wife team working on the project. It's just a matter of getting funding for an extra salary."

"Thanks, Brad, that gives me a little more hope. How about Friday of next week for the seminar?"

"Thursday would be much better if you can arrange it. Not too many people around here on Fridays. They seem to think they're entitled to a three-day weekend every week, and I'd like your seminar to be well attended."

"Sure, Thursday is okay. I can get Tony to take my classes, I think."

"Good, we'll arrange for your plane ticket. We'll pay your per diem expenses later, after everything is added up, if that's all right. It's all set then?"

"All set, Brad. I really *am* excited, you know. I just hope it will all work out."

"So do I, and since I'm a perennial optimist, I think it will. There's someone in my office waiting to see me, Janice, so I'll say good-bye. I'll contact you again as soon as we have information on your plane ticket."

"Bye, Brad. See you next week."

As she replaced the receiver, Janice could feel elation transfusing through her body. It was as if someone had taken a syringe and injected her with a wonderful, warming substance that lifted her ego in some magical way. She wondered if something like this was what drug addicts felt after their "fix." If so, perhaps she could partially understand their addiction. Well, anyway, she had a lecture to worry about right now. There would be plenty of time for going giddy later on if and when things worked out as she hoped they would. But nothing was settled yet. And she was determined not to be disappointed if things didn't turn out.

Perhaps she had just enough time to phone Tony with the news before sticking her nose into her lecture notes.

TWENTY

It was Friday and Janice had come to school with Tony even though she had no classes. There was some committee work that she wanted to catch up on. Also, she expected to hear anytime about the position she had applied for, and the news would come either in her school mail or over her office telephone. She would like to get it over with one way or the other. Waiting was not one of Janice's strong points.

She had gone to Gainesville three weeks before to deliver her seminar. She felt that it had gone reasonably well. It had been well attended and she had received some very nice compliments from those who were there. Brad Figgins told her that everyone he had talked to was impressed, including the other committee members in charge of screening the candidates. Brad was probably helping her cause as much as he could. But he had also indicated that one of the other candidates had seriously impressed the committee as well.

It was almost noon when Janice finished the main part of the committee assignment. There was just a little more to do before the committee met on Monday. She could easily finish in about an hour's time. The mail should have come by now, and would probably have been sorted and placed in the mail boxes.

There was the usual junk mail in Janice's box, and several business size envelopes lying face down, any one of which could be what she was waiting for. Might as well sort it out right here in the mail room and get rid of the crap, she thought to herself. The fourth envelope down was from Gainesville. Janice looked at it for a moment, but did not open it. She placed it with the others and quickly inspected the advertisements that were pushing books, laboratory equipment, chemicals and whatnot. None of them interested her and she threw them all into the trash receptacle. Then she picked up the letters and went back to her office.

She could feel her heart beating hard as she sat down in her desk chair. She took her letter opener and slit open the envelope from Gainesville. The letter was from Brad. It said that Janice had been the runner-up for the position, but someone else had beaten her. The other person had some experience in tropical research, and that had impressed the committee members. Brad felt badly about the outcome, but thanked Janice for applying. It had been so close.

Janice could do nothing to control the emotion. The sinking feeling, the instant depression and helplessness—she had been through it all before. But she knew that she would feel better in a few hours. The mind had a way of healing itself, and she was determined not to show her disappointment to Tony, who would be coming down the hall in a few minutes to eat lunch with her. She had done her best and that was all she could have done. Perhaps Tony would be happily relieved. Janice wasn't sure just how he felt about this matter. He was so inscrutable at times. Often she had wondered whether he was play-acting his enthusiasm for her application for the position. It would be just like him to hide his real feelings just to support her. Maybe it was all for the best that it hadn't happened.

When Tony came through the door he sensed immediately what she was going to tell him.

"Bad news, huh?" he said. Janice stared at him in wonderment.

"Sometimes you scare me, Tony. How could you have known?"

"Your face told me," he stated sadly. "I just knew when I first looked at you. I'm so sorry, Janice. I really hoped you would get that job. I was looking forward to it as much as you. What an adventure it would have been."

He took her in his arms and gave her a long, lingering kiss. He held her so tightly it almost hurt. When he released her, her eyes were swimming, but not from pain.

"Were you honestly looking forward to it?" she asked, "or were you just pretending for my sake?"

"No, I certainly wasn't pretending. I'm truly sorry that it didn't happen. Did Figgins call you?"

"No, I got a letter from him. I came in second. But he said it was close, if that's any satisfaction. Just a matter of this other guy having had more experience than I. Well, at least I know now, and things can settle down a little."

That evening immediately after dinner was over the phone rang. Jennifer had just begun washing the dinner dishes and Mickey, the cat, was happily chewing on some leftovers in his dish on the kitchen floor. Todd, who happened to be nearest the phone, answered it. He was expecting a call from a classmate—something about a math assignment for Monday.

"Mom, it's for you," he called.

"Who is it?"

"I don't know."

"I'll take it in the bedroom."

"Hello, this is Janice," she said to the phone receiver.

"Janice, this is Brad Figgins. Did you get a letter from me

today?" He sounded a little strange. Was he excited or something?

"Yes, I did."

"I was afraid you had. Well, scrap the letter." Janice sucked in her breath.

"It's good news," he said. "The candidate that the committee chose for the tropics position notified the committee chairman late this evening that he would have to turn it down. Said his wife rebelled; changed her mind about moving to the tropics. I was notified just a few minutes ago, and I thought you would want to know right away."

Janice was stunned. "Brad, are you serious?" she finally managed to gasp into the phone.

"I sure am. I couldn't wait till tomorrow morning to phone you. But then, it's still early in the evening where you are, isn't it. I keep forgetting the time difference. It's bedtime here."

"Brad, I can't believe it!" Janice had sat down on the bed because she wasn't sure her legs would hold her body up. "I just can't believe it."

"Well, it's true and I'm very happy for you if it's really what you want. I surely hope you will accept the appointment. I know you're just the right person for it."

After Janice had replaced the receiver, she was silent for a few moments. Then she let out a squeal that reverberated throughout the house. Mickey, the cat, scrambled for the backdoor with a frightened look on his face. Janice ran from the bedroom into the living room, where Jennifer, Todd and Tony had assembled, wondering what was going on.

"Guess what!" Janice cried.

"You got the job after all," replied Tony.

"How did you know that?"

"It's on your face, Janice. Written all over it," Tony responded.

There was so much to be done. The house had to be put up for sale. A wedding had to be performed. These were a couple of the big things. A million other little things, more or less, had to be accomplished also. Both Tony and Janice began making lists as they thought of details that could not be forgotten. What should Janice do with her furniture? Ship it all to Florida? Sell some of it? What about the two automobiles? Try to sell one? What about all their books. Which would go to Florida? Which to Central America? What should they do with the cat? It was maddening!

After talking to Dick Michaels, the department chairman, they both decided to take a year's leave of absence rather than resigning outright. That way, if for any reason the new situation did not work out for them, they could at least return to their present positions. They could resign at the end of another year.

The wedding took place in late May. As planned, it was a small affair in Janice's house. The parents of the bride and groom flew in from Northern California and Ohio respectively. It was the first time that Tony's parents had seen California. Tony picked them up at the Ontario Airport about 4:10 on a Friday afternoon. He drove them home on Interstate 10. Going west toward Los Angeles the Interstate was crowded but still moving. Coming east out of Los Angeles, however, it was totally gridlocked. Nothing was moving. His parents were absolutely astounded. They had never seen congestion like this. Tony's father vowed that he would never attempt to drive on a California freeway. Tony tried to explain that they weren't all quite this bad.

The two children were reacting differently to the move. Jennifer apparently didn't know what to make of it. Not until it was decided that Mickey, the cat, would return on the plane to Northern California with Grandma and Grandpa, did Jennifer realize that what was happening would affect her drastically. She cried. Janice cried with her, but there was really no alternative. At least they knew that Mickey would be well cared for. Todd was walking on air. He was simply ecstatic. It was *the* great adventure as far as he was concerned. His closest friends were envious, of course, and this made it all the better. Janice was happy for him. Todd would adjust to anything that might come up and would love every minute of it. Jennifer would be different. Janice knew there were going to be some difficult times ahead for her daughter. At least she had adjusted to her mother's marriage. She showed no animosity toward Tony. In fact, she had begun calling him "Dad" instead of Tony. At first it was a joke, but already it was starting to sound normal. Janice hadn't told Jennifer that Central America has earthquakes just like California, nor that Florida has hurricanes.

It was difficult saying good-bye to Nancy and Florence Granger and the four younger children. Janice had come to love them all. They promised each other that they would correspond regularly.

A farewell party was given by the Biology Department for the departing pair a week after the wedding. It was a happy-sad affair like most farewells. Several of the faculty expressed the wish to Janice that they could go with her. She had the feeling that they were not just trying to make conversation. They really meant it.

As she crawled into bed that night she thought about her own willingness to leave California. She had been born here and grew up here. It was all she knew. But she had seen changes she didn't like. She was afraid they were irreversible changes. Yes, it was time to leave. Thousands of other people apparently thought so too. She turned off the lights, settled down on her pillow and stared into the darkness. "Good-bye, California, no longer golden," she whispered to herself. "A deathwind has swept through and scattered your gold. You may never find it again."

Then Janice snuggled up against the already sleeping Tony, closed her eyelids and dropped off to sleep.